PRAISE FOR
SEVENTH GRADE VS. THE GALAXY

"A perfect bridge for readers looking for a Percy Jackson–esque work of science fiction."

—*School Library Journal*

"Levy writes humorous, fast-paced adventure that will take readers totally out of this world."

—Liesl Shurtliff, *New York Times* bestselling author of the Time Castaways trilogy

"Fast, fun, and freaking hilarious. . . . Levy's inventive, star-bright writing keeps the plot galloping and the jokes flying . . . You'll love *Seventh Grade vs. the Galaxy!*"

—Carlos Hernandez, author of *Sal and Gabi Break the Universe* and *Sal and Gabi Fix the Universe*

"In a hilarious, pitch-perfect voice, Joshua Levy delivers an action-packed adventure that is at once out of this world and entirely relatable. *Seventh Grade vs. the Galaxy* is hands down one of the most exciting debuts of 2019!"

—Jarrett Lerner, author of the EngiNerds series

"A total blast! Between hilarious space shenanigans and page-turning action, fun comes at you faster than a dodgeball!"

—Katie Slivensky, author of *The Countdown Conspiracy* and *The Seismic Seven*

"An unpredictable, laugh-out-loud-funny adventure wrapped in a mystery and set in a universe where middle school is even more complicated than it is on Earth."

—Chris Tebbetts, coauthor of *Middle School: The Worst Years of My Life* and *Middle School: Get Me Out of Here!*

"A stellar adventure filled with humor, heart, and lots of intergalactic antics!"
—Monica Tesler, author of the Bounders series

"An exciting adventure full of humor and action that will make you wish you went to school in space."

—Gareth Wronski, author of *Holly Farb and the Princess of the Galaxy*

EIGHTH GRADE vs. THE MACHINES

CAROLRHODA BOOKS
MINNEAPOLIS

Carolrhoda Books™
An imprint of Lerner Publishing Group, Inc.
241 First Avenue North
Minneapolis, MN 55401 USA

For reading levels and more information, look up this title at www.lernerbooks.com.

Cover illustration by Petur Antonsson.
Design element by Triff/Shutterstock.com (galaxy).

Main body text set in Bembo Std.
Typeface provided by Monotype Typography.

Library of Congress Cataloging-in-Publication Data

Names: Levy, Joshua (Joshua S.), author.
Title: Eighth grade vs. the machines / by Joshua S. Levy.
Other titles: Eighth grade versus the machines
Description: Minneapolis : Carolrhoda Books, [2021] | Audience: Ages 9–13. | Audience: Grades 7–9. | Summary: "The entire population of Earth's solar system has been kidnapped by aliens. It's up to Jack and his classmates and teachers aboard the PSS 118 to rescue the rest of humanity". —Provided by publisher.
Identifiers: LCCN 2020012588 (print) | LCCN 2020012589 (ebook) | ISBN 9781541598942 | ISBN 9781728417424 (ebook)
Subjects: CYAC: Adventure and adventurers—Fiction. | Space ships—Fiction. | Schools—Fiction. | Extraterrestrial beings—Fiction. | Kidnapping—Fiction. | Science fiction. | Humorous stories.
Classification: LCC PZ7.1.L4895 Eig 2021 (print) | LCC PZ7.1.L4895 (ebook) | DDC [Fic]—dc23

LC record available at https://lccn.loc.gov/2020012588
LC ebook record available at https://lccn.loc.gov/2020012589

Manufactured in the United States of America
1-48071-48743-5/11/2021

Another one for Tali, Serena, and Henry.

PUBLIC SCHOOL SPACESHIP 118 EIGHTH GRADE WEEKLY SCHEDULE: FALL SEMESTER

PERIOD	TIME	MONDAY	TUESDAY	WEDNESDAY
	8:00am EST* – 8:35am	Homeroom *Mrs. Diehr & Andy Campbell*	Homeroom *Dr. Hazelwood*	Homeroom *Mrs. Diehr & Andy Campbell*
1	8:38am – 9:23am	Social Studies: History of the Jovian Sector, Galileo Orbiter (1995) to Treaty of Amalthea (2233) *Mr. Cardegna*	Social Studies: History of the Jovian Sector, Galileo Orbiter (1995) to Treaty of Amalthea (2233) *Mr. Cardegna*	Social Studies: History of the Jovian Sector, Galileo Orbiter (1995) to Treaty of Amalthea (2233) *Mr. Cardegna*
2	9:25am – 10:10am	Science: Intermediate Thermonuclear Physics *Mrs. Watts*	Science: Intermediate Thermonuclear Physics (Lab) *Mrs. Watts*	Science: Intermediate Thermonuclear Physics *Mrs. Watts*
	10:10am – 10:35am	Morning Recess (Gym)	Morning Recess (Military Park, if planetside)	Morning Recess (Gym)
3	10:35am – 11:20am	Language Arts *Mr. Cardegna*	Language Arts *Mr. Cardegna*	Language Arts *Mr. Cardegna*
4	11:23am – 12:08pm	Rudimentary Flight Skills I: PSS 118 Mechanics & Maneuverability *Captain Little & the Ship*	Intro to Alien Defense *Ms. Needle*	Rudimentary Flight Skills II: Small Craft & Personal Propulsion Devices *Principal Lochner & Ms. Needle*
	12:08pm – 12:50pm	Lunch (Printed)	Lunch (Fresh)	Lunch (Printed)
	12:50 – 1:15pm	Afternoon Recess (Military Park, if planetside)	Afternoon Recess (Gym)	Afternoon Recess (Military Park, if planetside)
5	1:15pm – 2:00pm	Language Elective *Mrs. Diehr (Group A)* *Ms. Needle (Group B)* *Principal Lochner (Group C)*	Geography (Astronomical) *Mr. Cardegna*	Language Elective *Mrs. Diehr (Group A)* *Ms. Needle (Group B)* *Principal Lochner (Group C)*
6	2:03pm – 2:48pm	Math: Pre-Quantum Field Theory *Ms. Needle*	Math: Pre-Quantum Field Theory *Ms. Needle*	Math: Pre-Quantum Field Theory *Ms. Needle*
7	2:51pm – 3:36pm	P.E. (Gym) *Andy Campbell*	Art/Music Elective *Ms. Needle (Group A)* *Andy Campbell (Group B)*	P.E. (Ship Maintenance) *Georgia Hawkes*
	3:45pm – 4:30pm	Clubs/Sports/Activities	Clubs/Sports/Activities	Clubs/Sports/Activities

THURSDAY	FRIDAY
Homeroom	Homeroom
Dr. Hazelwood	*Mrs. Diehr & Andy Campbell*
Social Studies: History of the Jovian Sector, Galileo Orbiter (1995) to Treaty of Amalthea (2233)	Social Studies: History of the Jovian Sector, Galileo Orbiter (1995) to Treaty of Amalthea (2233)
Mr. Cardegna	*Mr. Cardegna*
Science: Intermediate Thermonuclear Physics (Lab)	Science: Intermediate Thermonuclear Physics
Mrs. Watts	*Mrs. Watts*
Morning Recess (Military Park, if planetside)	Morning Recess (Gym)
Language Arts	Language Arts
Mr. Cardegna	*Mr. Cardegna*
Intro to Alien Defense	Intro to Alien Defense
Ms. Needle	*Ms. Needle*
Lunch (Fresh)	Lunch (Printed)
Afternoon Recess (Gym)	Afternoon Recess (Military Park, if planetside)
Geography (Terrestrial)	Geography (Astronomical)
Mr. Cardegna	*Mr. Cardegna*
Math: Pre-Quantum Field Theory	Math: Pre-Quantum Field Theory
Ms. Needle	*Ms. Needle*
Library	Leadership Training Seminar
Mrs. Diehr	*Principal Lochner & Dr. Hazelwood*
Clubs/Sports/Activities	Clubs/Sports/Activities

FALL INTRAMURAL SPORTS
Basketball**
Tennis**
Soccer**
Track***

**In 1 G when planetside.
***No 0 G track team this year.

Go PSS 118 Champions!

FALL CLUBS/ACTIVITIES
Debate

A/V

Newspaper
(*PSS 118 Star-Ledger*)

Chess
(three- and four-dimensional)

Glee

Drama
(Shakespeare in Space;
fall semester will feature a musical)

Lightyearbook Committee

Shop
(Nanoprinter Coding)

Book Club
(theme: Holographic Novels are Novels!)

Student Council
(outgoing Pres. Mississippi Tinker;
elections in November)

ART/MUSIC ELECTIVE CHOICES
(groups to switch for spring semester)
Group A: Art of Earth
Group B: Evolution of Moon Rock

LANGUAGE ELECTIVE CHOICES
(full year)
Group A: Advanced Arabic
Group B: Intermediate Spanish
Group C: Elvidian as a Second Language

NAME: _____

*U.S. Eastern Standard Time = -7 hrs. from JST
(Jupiter Standard Time)

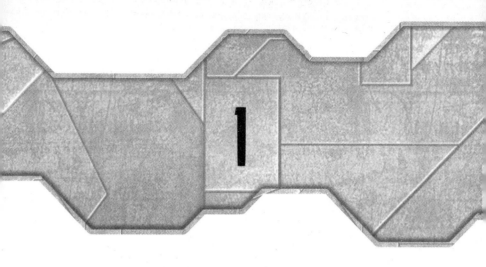

1

Listen. I don't have a lot of time. So I'll catch you up quick. Humanity's missing. My dad invented a light speed engine on our schoolship, which drew some . . . unwanted attention, alienwise. Now we're the only ones left: a middle school from Ganymede, stuck on Earth, no idea where to go next. And—oh yeah—we're in the middle of maybe the most important battle this planet has ever seen.

"I know you're in here, Jack!" my enemy says, chomping down on her gum and popping a bubble. "It's over. Time for the great Jacksonville Graham to surrender."

I'm stuck inside one of New York's empty sky-scrapers, crouching behind a giant column, listening to footsteps slowly *click clack* across the room. Every sound boom-echoes through this lobby. Between its gold-plated walls. Up to its high ceilings carved with images of the city.

"Come out, come out, wherever you are," she calls.

I tilt my body farther back into the corner, trying to minimize my shadow. Hiding is harder than you'd think, given the bulky contraption on my back. It grazes the column with an unfortunate clank.

"You know you can't escape."

She's right. I'll never make it past her to the exit. Every approach to the doors puts me in her line of fire. But there has to be a way out. There's *always* a way out.

I peek around the column to survey my options: A gift shop, maybe twenty feet away. Public restrooms on either end of the main atrium. A set of escalators, still running smoothly even after the world has ended. And a bank of five elevators on the opposite wall, each with a different destination carved into an adjacent silver plate:

FLOORS 4 THROUGH 49.

FLOORS 50 THROUGH 99.

FLOORS 100 THROUGH 149.

FLOORS 150 THROUGH 199.

OUTDOOR OBSERVATION DECK: 175th FLOOR.

There's also a space elevator that leaves from the mezzanine, just behind the escalators: "With stops at 100,000km, 200,000km, and the Lagrange Point 1 Resort and Spa." But that's probably overkill. All I need is to get to that observation deck. Then I'll be able to—

Zwamb. The sound of her laser rifle powering up.

"Surrender!" she shouts. "To the superior skills of Beckenham Pierce!"

Becka and me. On opposite sides.

I take a deep breath, kicking myself for losing my own laser blaster somewhere uptown.

At least I've still got my Pencil—a portable 3D nanoprinter. Last year, my best friend, Ari Bowman, hacked the source code, which allowed his school Pencil to print basically anything. When he eventually fessed up to Principal Lochner, we thought Ari's Pencil would get confiscated for sure. Instead the teachers agreed to let the rest of us eighth graders have unrestricted Pencils too. They even maxed out the number of nanobots each Pencil carries. If it's up to us to save humanity, we can at least have nice things.

I click and start writing in the air. Ari and I joined after-school shop club this year and have been preprogramming all sorts of apps into our Pencils. That way you don't need to code everything out. You can just write keywords in the air. Click. And out pops your creation. We've programmed some practical stuff, like *MAG-BOOTS* and *HYPERSONIC EARBUDS*. And some not-so-practical options: *ZERO-G SLIP-AND-SLIDE* (warning: very dangerous) and *HAMSTER MECH* (for Ari's pet, Doctor Shrew, who can jump like ten feet in the air when Ari straps him into the tiny exoskeleton). Ari's got a bunch more programs in development: *TRACKER BUG. LIE DETECTOR. MUFFIN TINS.*

"Heeeeere, Jackie, Jackie," Becka calls out, sweeping her laser rifle's scope back and forth across the lobby. A red dot whizzes around the room.

She's getting closer. Becka's like a foot taller than me. And from my hiding place, I can see the top of her hair, which she's dyed pitch black.

Click. A five-foot-long creation materializes. I gently position it behind me, leaning against the column. Take my communicator ring off my finger and find a voice recording to play. Set a timer for five seconds and slide it underneath the mass of disguised nanorobots.

Becka crosses the lobby, pointing her blaster at the back of what I made with the Pencil. "Are you really just hiding in a corner? That's kind of pathetic, even for you."

"Rude," I grumble, making a quiet run for it— around the column, toward the elevators.

My ring blurts out the recording: "This is Jack! Sorry my family brought on the apocalypse! Leave a message at the beep!"

And Becka goes, "Gotcha now!"

Except I'm already across the lobby. I press the button, press the button, press the button—*come on!*—and finally, one elevator opens with a loud *ding!*

Becka whiplashes her head around, shouting, "What the . . . argh!"

She grabs my nanobot creation—a giant foam doll— and throws it to the ground.

"Are you kidding me?!" she shrieks, kicking the doll for good measure. There's a *pop* and a long wheezing sound, like a balloon fizzing air through a tiny hole. "You used your nanobot replica?! That's cheating!"

I smile. *Pencil Program: DECOY JACK.* It's a perfect copy—same light hair, same freckly skin, same awkwardly large bug-eyes. The program is even designed to scan me and come out dressed in whatever clothes I'm wearing. Which today—with the new, "relaxed" dress code—means jeans and a plaid button-down.

We have a light speed engine. We've traveled through time and space and fought aliens bent on galactic domination. And still, Principal Lochner defines the line between civilization and chaos as "collared shirts."

Becka shoots rapid-fire pulses at me. I duck just in time, and the elevator doors close. But not before I cup my hands against my mouth and yell, "It's not cheating!"

Because it's not! There're only like six rules to this whole game. All's fair in Jetpack Lasertag Capture-the-Flag.

The elevator doors open again, and I yawn to pop my ears. It's bright up here—all windows and sunshine. I'm alone except for a powered-down robot that sits behind an information booth. The robot wears a baseball cap that reads: *EXPRESS FERRIES EVERY FIFTEEN MINUTES TO BROOKLYN, FAR ROCKAWAY, AND THE MOON.* I hop over waiting-line ropes and dash past the booth, following arrows pointing me to the observation deck. By the time—*ding!*—Becka's elevator arrives, I'm outside. But Becka's fast. Faster than me. I'm cornered in seconds.

"There's nowhere to run," she says. "Give me the flag and I'll tell everyone else on your team that you fought bravely."

I grin. The observation deck is fenced in on all sides but open at the top to the clear blue sky. Through the mesh fence, I can see past midtown, down the length of Central Park. Somewhere to the west—along the riverfront in downtown Newark—our ship is waiting.

She flicks my comm ring over to me. I catch it and put it back on my finger.

"Thanks," I say. "But who said anything about *running?*"

I stomp my right foot twice, activating the jetpack on my back as Becka fires a laser shot right where I'm standing. Or right where I *was* standing.

I shoot up into the air, spiraling wildly like a misshapen corkscrew. But after a few seconds, I steady out. All that practice has been helping, I guess. I yank the over-the-shoulder clutch and turn sharply around the side of the building. As I zoom west toward New Jersey, two of my teammates fly up alongside me.

"Where've you been?!" I yell at Ari.

"Sorry!" says Missi Tinker. "We got pinned down in Times Square." That's where Becka and her team hid their flag. While everyone was distracted, Ari sent in a

7

mechanized Doctor Shrew. He got the flag out. (I mean, technically, the AI exoskeleton did most of the work, but still.) Swapped it for a decoy without anyone noticing. Got it to me. And I rocketed downtown. According to Principal Lochner, the winning team gets "the most important prize there is."

And. I. Think. We. Are. Going. To. Win.

A laser bolt shoots past my left ear. I glance back. Becka's hot on our tail, now flanked by her sister, Diana, and our classmate Riya Windsor. They both pull out their laser blasters and start firing at us.

"Scatter!" Missi shouts, and we do. But it's too late. She's hit almost immediately, caught in the crossfire.

"Missi!" Ari screams, dramatically reaching out a hand. But she can't help us anymore. She's out of the game and has to return to the ship at quarter speed.

"Keep going!" Missi shouts, as we leave her behind.

The last few months have been pretty intense. My dad's light speed engine summoned the Quarantine, an alien teleportation device that disappeared everyone in the solar system. Meanwhile, our school got stranded light years away from home. We escaped the clutches of the Minister, a super-evil alien queen, and crash-landed on Earth. Leaving it to us—the kids and grown-ups of the Public School Spaceship 118—to track down our fellow humans and bring them home.

And if you're thinking: *Hey, Jack, with all that, who cares whether you win or lose some silly game?* Well, you've obviously never played a game against Becka "T-Bex" Pierce, have you?

A laser bolt flies past me from up ahead. More of Becka's teammates—Hunter, Madison, and Kinston—are rocketing toward us.

We're almost there. But we're not close enough. The sky lights up with crisscrossing laser fire and the only way to go is—

"Down!" Ari screams, and I follow.

The streets in this part of the city are narrow and meet at awkward angles. When we hit the ground in the middle of one of these intersections, chills run down my spine. And not just because there's a late-fall breeze in the air. This ghost town still gives me the creeps. Skulking around inside an empty lobby is one thing. But out here, surrounded by so many skyscrapers and so much silence . . . you never quite get used to it.

"There's got to be somewhere to hide," I say, pulling Ari toward the subway stairs. Maybe we can wait them out. Or find a way through the tunnels, even if the vac-trains aren't running. But we only manage to take three steps forward before—*slam*—Becka lands right in front us, smirking from ear to ear.

Slam. Slam. Diana and Riya land on either side of her. They form a semicircle, blocking our way into the station. We turn to run in the opposite direction. But—

Slam. Slam. Slam.

Hunter. Madison. Kingston. Closing the circle. Surrounding us. Even if we activate our jetpacks again, we're bound to take blaster fire.

Becka extends her hand. "Give me the flag and nobody has to get hurt."

I grit my teeth. Losing to Becka. Again.

"Just shoot me," I tell her, crossing my arms. "Then I'll turn the flag over. I'm not out till I'm out."

"Suit yourself," she says, lifting her weapon.

Zwamb.

Someone beats her to it. But instead of hearing the chime on *my* wrist monitor—which tells you when you've been hit—Becka's goes off. Diana's and Riya's too.

"What?!" Becka shrieks, ripping off her monitor and chucking it to the ground. "Why?!"

I turn toward the focus of her wrath. Hunter, Madison, and Kingston. Blasters raised. Grins plastered on their faces.

Hunter shrugs. "That's for last week." Another volley in his and Becka's ongoing prank war, which gets closer to an actual war every day.

"But we're on the same team!" Becka says. "I picked you!"

Hunter laughs. "Well, that was a mistake, wasn't it? You should know by now that *my* favorite game is seeing your face when you lose."

"When *we* lose!" she corrects, howling into the sky.

"Um," I say to Hunter, "does this mean we can go?"

"Be my guest. They can't fire on you." Hunter nods at Becka. Next he shoots his own wrist monitor. Madison's and Kingston's too. "Now we can't either."

Ari and I look at each other. Is this really happening?

"*Now* it's cheating," Becka declares, marching up to Ari and me. "Don't go along with it. Don't give Hunter the satisfaction. It's not a fair win. You can, um . . . forfeit! Yeah! Forfeit the game. And we'll call it a tie."

Pre-apocalypse Ari would totally have caved to Becka. Post-apocalypse Ari makes a face like he's tempted to cave, but shrugs instead. "Better luck next time?"

The blasts of our rocket boosters drown out whatever Becka shouts next. I glance down as we fly: She's in Hunter's face now, waving her arms back and forth. Hunter is beaming.

Up in the sky, Ari and I zoom across the river, toward our ship, the faithful(ish) PSS 118. We land in the grassy riverfront park. Our classmates are waiting for us, and half the school erupts with cheers when I pull the other team's flag out of my pocket. Principal Locher's voice rings out through the ship's comms as he calls the game. He's onboard the 118, watching from the brand new command bridge.

"Congrats, Jack! Now get inside, everyone! No time to lose. I sincerely hope you all enjoyed your last day on Earth."

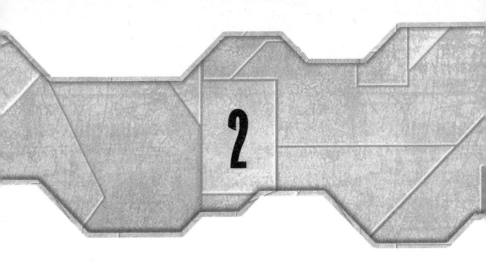

2

Ari's convinced that we're going to be legends. He's been saying it for months, ever since we arrived on Earth. "You'll see," he told me just this morning, before the game started. "After we save everyone, they'll, like, build museums about the 118. Everything we do now is important. It sets *precedent*." Which is a word I'm one hundred percent sure Ari did not know before we were abducted by aliens.

I grabbed Ari's journal, opened to a random page, and read out loud in the deepest voice I could muster. "Ari's Log. Day 93. We had scrambled eggs again for breakfast. With cheese. But I had eggs yesterday. (See Day 92.) And they were good. But cheesy eggs two days in a row, you know? Rough on the ol' tumtum. So I made myself a peanut butter sandwich instead. Main toaster was broken. Used secondary toaster."

I looked up. "What would future generations do without this crucial historical information?"

Ari snatched the journal back. "It's usually more interesting than that." He flipped pages and read from random entries. "Day 98: Flight training. Day 101: Rail gun testing. Day 107 . . ."

Technically, the journal is a project for Mr. Cardegna's language arts class. Some are taking the assignment seriously. Others aren't. See if you can guess which category Ari's in, based on the sparkly title of his Pencil-printed notebook: *Lost & Found: The Daily Logs of Arizona Bowman—True Tales of Aliens, Light Speed, And Time Travel. An Autobiography: The Arizona Bowman Story.*

I peeked over Ari's shoulder. "Day 108," I read. "Went to the park today. Was a nice day. Sat in grass."

Ari slammed the book closed. "It *was* a nice day! Anyway, you'll see: When we find everyone, your journal will be useless and our fellow humans will thank me for every detail."

Of course, that assumes there will eventually be a "they" to do the thanking.

Ari's been a confidence supernova since we started rebuilding the ship. He's absolutely positive that nothing can stop us. Me? I'm not so sure. In those first weeks after planetfall, I was right there with him. But weeks turned to months. And the months dragged on. And . . . I can't help it. I'm a little less sure than I used to be. Less certain that we can really make a difference.

***

". . . because really," Principal Lochner is saying, "isn't friendship the greatest prize of all? The prize of enjoying a day with people you care about?"

A few kids laugh. Mostly kids on the other team. At the back of the cafeteria—which Ari now insists on calling the mess hall, "because it's more epic that way"—someone boos. Though on second thought, that might have been the ship itself.

I for one am glad that there's no prize for winning the game. Maybe it'll make Becka less mad. I crane my neck to look at her, sitting at the end of the front row instead of in the middle with Ari and me. No luck. She's still rage-cracking her knuckles, one at a time. Always a bad sign.

"Today is a big day," Principal Lochner continues, as if we didn't already know. "I'm glad that you all got to bask in a little sun. No telling when the next chance will come along."

It feels like we've been waiting forever to be ready. Repairing and upgrading the PSS 118 was bound to take time. With only a hundred middle schoolers and ten adults (most of them teachers), we're not exactly an army of engineers. But still. Six months? They're out there, somewhere. It's our job to find them. Our friends. Our families. My mom and dad. And we've been stuck here for *six months*.

* * *

14

"Why do you think you are so impatient to start our mission *and* so concerned that we are going to fail?" Dr. Hazelwood asked me at last week's session. Principal Lochner makes sure we each have a weekly check-in with the school guidance counselor.

"I don't know . . . my dad?" I answered—because maybe that's true. But it also happens to be the easiest way to get Dr. Hazelwood off my back. One mention of former science teacher slash intergalactic criminal Allentown Graham is usually all it takes for Dr. H to talk at me for five whole minutes. Which is so much better than having to answer more questions.

"That makes perfect sense. As we've discussed, although you are not responsible for your father's actions—building the light speed engine, triggering the Quarantine—you still feel the weight of their consequences. Setting low expectations is a perfectly natural defense mechanism against the heartbreak that comes with failure. Even though that heartbreak won't actually be lessened by pessimism." He paused to breathe, then asked: "And why do you think that is?"

"I don't know . . . my mom?" I answered, which got him going for another three whole minutes. Before the light speed engine and the aliens, she left my dad and me for a new doctor job on Earth. A topic that's totally unrelated to our mission. But another sure-fire way to get Dr. Hazelwood to run out the clock.

***

"I know we've had some setbacks," Principal Lochner continues as our preflight assembly drags on. Somewhere behind me, Hunter cackles. I can't really blame him. *Some setbacks* is the understatement of the light year. Like the time we finished repairing the inner hull and it sprang a giant leak when it rained the next day. Or the first test flight, with just Principal Lochner and the ship's crew—Harriet, Tim, and Georgia. The 118 got maybe ten thousand feet into the air before it crashed. Or the time we remote-tested the new close-range cannons and *the command bridge exploded.*

"But we're ready now. We have to be ready now. The rest of humanity is counting on us. So let's go over the plan one more time, shall we? Thanks to Jack, Becka, and Ari, we have our map."

It's true. Last year, when we were on the run from the Minister, we got ahold of a map of the Elvid System. Lucky for us, it also included data on every known populated planet in the galaxy.

"*AHEM,*" the ship chimes in.

Principal Lochner rolls his eyes. "Yes. And it was our very own not-at-all-narcissistic ship's AI that plotted the alien map against the limited star charts available from the Library of Congress."

"*YOU'RE WELCOME,*" the 118 says.

Principal Lochner dims the lights and brings up the

now-familiar hologram of the galaxy. He first zooms in on our own solar system, along one of the spinoffs of the Orion-Cygnus Arm. (Mr. Cardegna's been pushing us hard in Astronomical Geography lately. Test me: 3kpc, Perseus, Norma, Outer, New Outer, Scutum-Centaurus, Carina-Sagittarius, and Orion-Cygnus. Mr. Cardegna's mnemonic device helps: Three Purple Ninjas Outwitted Nine Scary Carnivorous Octopi.)

"This," Principal Lochner zooms out and back in along Carina-Sagittarius, "is the Wyzard System."

At least that's what the Elvidian map calls it. It's just a name. It doesn't necessarily mean that . . . well . . . actually . . . who knows? When I started seventh grade, there was no such thing as light speed engines or aliens or time travel. So maybe magic exists and we're heading toward a solar system full of alien wizards. Ari's already stored a pile of fancy capes in his dorm room just in case.

"The Wyzard System," Principal Lochner continues, "is home to the largest and most comprehensive library in the galaxy. Our first stop on what may be a very long journey. If there is information to be learned about the Quarantine—specifically, where it may have sent our fellow humans—we'll find it there. Just like with any research assignment, we're going to start at the library."

Missi Tinker's hand immediately shoots up.

"Yes, Mississippi?"

"What if the Minister shows up? Attacks us or sends us away?"

He nods. "I won't lie to you and say that I don't worry about the exact same thing. But we're as prepared as we can be. In some ways, this may look a lot like the old 118—"

"*WHO YOU CALLING OLD?*"

"My apologies." Principal Lochner pats the wall with sarcastic affection. "This may look a lot like the *ancient* 118."

"*HAR HAR.*"

"But it's not the same vessel it was when we arrived. You've each contributed to outfitting our little schoolship with some of the most advanced technology humankind has to offer. Dual-reinforced graphene-composite hull paneling. External particle-deflector shields. Multiple weapons systems. I can't promise we'll be any match for what's to come. But this time, we have a fighting chance."

* * *

We spent the whole summer rebuilding the ship. And the day after Labor Day: a new school year. Eighth grade. Mr. Cardegna enthusiastically teaching social studies and language arts. Mrs. Watts crankily teaching science. Like nothing had changed. Until fourth period.

"We're calling this class Introduction to Alien Defense," Ms. Needle announced, calling up the new holographic simulator we'd installed in Classroom 4.

"AKA weapons training," Becka whispered to Ari and me.

"This is *defense*," Ms. Needle stressed. "Weapons are a last resort. In the first few weeks, we'll cover some basic martial arts techniques. For Unit Two, we'll train with the laser rifles—"

Becka squealed.

"Stun only," Ms. Needle added. "And even then, not until every single one of you has passed a comprehensive safety examination—"

"Ugh," Riya groaned.

"Tell me about it," Becka mumbled.

"—and in-person evaluations with both Principal Lochner and Dr. Hazelwood. *Then* we'll begin running drills. I'm including a week on the new electrostatic grenade launchers—"

"Awesome," Ari whispered. I nodded.

"And I'm still trying to convince Principal Lochner that you should also learn some basic *systems* defense. At least the CRCs, maybe the rail guns too. Might have to save countermeasures for the spring semester. And—"

"Why are *you* teaching us defense?" Hunter interrupted. "Does being a gym teacher qualify you to shoot aliens out of the sky?"

"Shut up, Hunter," Becka and Riya said at the same time.

Ms. Needle's face wilted for a moment, then lifted. "No, that's a fair question. Even if asked rudely. The honest answer? I'm *not* qualified. But neither is anyone else onboard. So Principal Lochner has asked me to take on the responsibility. I've read countless books, articles, and manuals on these subjects. Spent hours in this simulator, every day, for two months. I designed all of the sims myself and won them all a hundred times over. And I know how to teach. Helping my students learn? Preparing them for what's out there in the universe? *That* is something I'm very qualified to do."

The room was silent. Everyone was convinced. (Except maybe Hunter. But at least he kept quiet.)

"Any other questions before we dive in?"

Just one:

"Yes, Becka?"

"So this class . . . is something you can *win*?"

* * *

Principal Lochner smiles down at us from the podium. There's a faint round of clapping. This isn't our first pep talk/assembly, and the applause is weaker than it used to be. I'm not the only one who isn't so confident anymore. But Ari is cheering. So are Riya and Missi and Ming Elfbrandt. And Becka, of course. I lean forward and catch her grinning. If there's one thing that's always sure to cheer her up, it's talk of the weapons systems. Wanna guess who has the highest fall semester "win record" in Intro to Alien Defense?

"The Piercers!" Ari hoots, using Becka's term for the rail guns, which she named after herself.

"Frankly," Principal Lochner continues, "if the Minister wanted to come after us, she'd have done it by now, even with the planetary defense satellites on high alert. It's possible she has bigger fish to fry or—"

"Or she's waiting for us to come to her," Hunter interrupts. Seeing a pattern?

"Perhaps, Mr. LaFleur. But we can't stay here. It's time to go."

Hunter stands bolt upright. "Who said anything about staying here?"

"Hunter—"

"We've got the galaxy map, right? So let's explore the freaking galaxy!"

"Hunter—"

A few other kids nod along. Madison and Kingston, obviously. And a bunch of kids from the grades below us: Salina C., Salina P., Albi Butler, Leigh Lucia . . . even Diana Pierce. There's this weird Hunter following among some of the seventh graders. Every day a dozen of them trot after him in the hallway, holding his backpack, passing him cups of water, and arguing over who's got the privilege of stealing extra lunch rations for their bully-in-chief.

"Let's find the most fun place in the galaxy and relax before the Minister finds us and blasts us to wherever, or worse. Any place has to be better than"—Hunter shudders—"a library."

"Hunter," Principal Lochner says sharply, "that's enough. Sit down. We have a mission. We have *family*. We're going to find them and bring them home. That is the only option."

"Whatever," Hunter grumbles.

I do not envy Principal Lochner's job. If this was last year, he could've at least called Hunter's parents. (Even though that never helped. The LaFleurs usually spent back-to-school night sneering at the teachers. The moon doesn't orbit far from the planet, if you know what I mean.) Before the Quarantine, Hunter could've been suspended or expelled. Now there's nowhere else for him to go. And ever since we crashed, Hunter's been collecting detentions like they're badges of honor.

Principal Lochner clears his throat. "If there are no more questions, it's time to set out for the stars."

It's a little melodramatic, maybe, but nobody laughs. I look to my left. Ari's feet are bouncing up and down. And all the way back over to my right, Becka's eyes are narrowed with concentration as if she's staring the Minister in the face, daring her to come after us.

Principal Lochner touches something on the screen of his podium to lower it back into the floor. Then he takes his center seat in the row of admin and teacher chairs, which line the back wall of the lunchroom, facing the kids.

"Okay, everyone," he says. "Buckle up."

A hundred simultaneous *clicks* bounce around the cafeteria—sorry, the mess hall. Over the summer, we ripped up the digital paper on the floor and bolted down heavy-duty chairs. Each seat has buckles and harnesses and NASA-grade launch/reentry foam. (And little pullout tables too, for, you know, actual lunch.) Folding chairs in space probably wasn't the best idea anyway.

"Harriet?" Principal Lochner says over the intercom. "Turn us on."

"Starting up the engines now," the captain replies from the bridge.

With a rumble, the PSS 118 Version 2.0 comes fully alive.

"YOU KNOW, I CAN DO THIS PART ALL BY MYSELF," the ship announces.

"I think Captain Little can handle it," Principal Lochner says.

"FAMOUS LAST WORDS."

"Too mean," Harriet says over the loudspeaker.

We're all laughing—because the more things change, the more they stay the same.

"Launch sequence initiating," Harriet responds. "Ten, nine, eight—"

It reminds me of the countdown that started all this. When the Quarantine first hit our solar system. When it failed to take *us* away, but took away almost everyone else we've ever cared about.

Except this countdown is different. This one is on our own terms.

Which is why, by the last few numbers, the whole school is counting down together.

"Four! Three! Two! One!"

The ship rises off the ground, and real hope bursts inside me for the first time in a long time.

Until we plop down, hard.

The power cuts out.

And the room goes dark, except for the red emergency lights running along the floor.

Yep. The more things change, the more they stay the same.

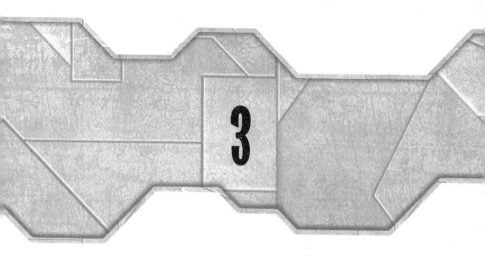

3

"I don't understand," Principal Lochner yells into the intercom. "We checked *everything*. We checked over and over."

The power has flickered back on, but the engines haven't. Mr. Cardegna and Ms. Needle are crowded around the principal's podium, staring at status reports on its screen. Behind them, Mrs. Watts is standing stiffly against the wall, arms crossed. In the back of the room, Dr. Hazelwood is trying to console a couple of bawling sixth graders. The only other non-crew adults with us are Jina Diehr (the school librarian), Mr. Hogan (the school nurse), and Andy I-always-forget-his-last-name (a college-aged student teacher who only comes out of his room to teach music class and gym class, probably because he was supposed to be interning on the 118 for a few weeks and not *the rest of his life*). They're still buckled into their seats, glassy-eyed, staring straight ahead.

"TOLD YOU THAT I SHOULD HAVE HAN-DLED THE LAUNCH," the 118 says.

Principal Lochner lowers the ship's volume. "Not helpful."

"It all worked fine an hour ago," Georgia, the ship's engineer, adds over the intercom.

"Yes, but right now—" Principal Lochner pauses, as if he's suddenly realized something important. And now he's actually smiling at us, the way he does on any ordinary day, when nothing's wrong. It's a totally believable smile that reaches all the way to his eyes, which makes me wonder whether that smile is always fake and something is always wrong.

"Why doesn't everyone take half an hour," he says. "Go to your dorms. Relax. We'll sort this out in no time and then we can be on our way."

Cue the groans as—way, way too soon—we unclick our seatbelts and scatter. Ari and I head to the end of our row, where Becka and Diana are huddled. We pass Hunter and his minions, complaining loudly about "our loser ship."

"Either way," Mr. Cardegna says, ushering the Hunter contingent out of the cafeteria, "don't forget that we're presenting excerpts from our journals tomorrow. Whether we're on the ground or in orbit—third period language arts class is promptly at 10:35 a.m."

"I don't know if you've noticed," Hunter spits, "but the world is kind of over. Not sure keeping diaries is gonna solve our problems."

"How fascinating," Mr. Cardegna responds good-naturedly. "I'll be sure to call on you first to share with us."

Which shuts Hunter up real quick. Every other Monday—between physics and rudimentary flight skills class—Mr. Cardegna has us read from our journals. To "process" how we're feeling. Ari lives for reading days. Becka's pretty into it too. But Hunter isn't exactly the reflective type. The last time he presented, he just showed us a blank sheet of paper, titled, *Life After Aliens*. Mr. Cardegna deemed it "bleak."

"Wanna go play Neptune Attacks?" I ask Ari, Becka, and her sister.

"Whatever," Diana says, even though I know she wants to play. Ari nods eagerly. But Becka . . .

"Ari," she says, "please tell Jack that playing games with him isn't fun anymore."

"Jack," Ari starts, "Becka says that playing—"

"I heard her!" Directly to Becka, I add, "Come on, you're serious? It's not *my* fault that Hunter didn't play fair. And besides, Ari got away from you too!"

"Ari," Becka says calmly, "please tell Jack that, while you might have also been on the winning team, it was Jack who had the flag. It was his call. Please also inform him that I'm not upset that Hunter's a jerk. That's just a fact. You can't be mad that the Sun is hot or whatever. I'm upset that *he*"—she jabs me in the chest—"didn't stand up for me."

"Jack," Ari repeats, "Becka says—"

I sigh. "I. Can. Hear. Her. It was just a game, Becka."

Her cheeks go red and she snorts like a bull about to charge. Wrong approach, Jack.

"Besides," I try, switching tactics, "everybody knows that if Hunter hadn't turned on you, you'd have totally gotten me out. I'm no match for you."

She fast-blinks a few times. I've softened her steely heart a little.

"Can we go to the common room and sort this out *while* we play?" Ari suggests. "If we're not quick, the Salinas are gonna hog all the good avatars."

So we shuffle down the hall toward the dorms, even Becka.

As we walk, passing the science and computer labs, Diana grumbles, "We're never getting off this planet. You know that, right?"

"You sound like Hunter," Becka says.

"Why's that a bad thing?"

Becka gapes at her. "Excuse me?! Since when do you take his side?"

Diana shrugs. "We're friends now, kind of."

"Friends?" Becka snorts in disgust. "I can't believe you. Hunter's never cared about another person in his entire life! He's the last person in the galaxy you should be listening to. Back me up, Ari."

I notice that she hasn't asked *me* for input. Maybe because she's still mad. Maybe because she knows that

I don't have the most faith in the teachers right now either.

"Definitely," Ari says, before immediately changing the subject. "Also, how about this?" He takes a deep breath. "May Sol burn brightly till the end."

I consider Ari's suggestion. "It's fine."

"I like it," Becka says.

Ari nods. "But do you like it better than the call-and-response where the leader shouts, 'The void is great!' and everyone else punches their chests and answers, 'But we are greater!' I'm also still partial to 'Children of Zeus, unite!' and—"

"What are you *saying*?" Diana asks as we pass the gym. We hear a few kids inside, calling for a pickup game of one-g basketball.

"Well," Ari explains, "Zeus was the ancient Greek name for Jupiter. And we're from the Jovian sector, so . . ."

"Ari's been workshopping catchphrases," Becka clarifies.

"Can't go on a space adventure without one. Something to say when the chips are down and the stakes are high. I'm also considering . . ." He rattles off five more suggestions before we step into the common room.

"—never getting us off this planet!" Hunter is screaming.

He's standing on the couch across from the foosball table. Madison and Kingston are on either side of him, arms crossed like bodyguards. He's shouting to a crowd of maybe thirty kids. At least half of them are nodding along.

Diana takes a few steps forward to join the crowd. But Becka puts a hand on her shoulder and squeezes, as if to say, *Not so far, okay?*

"Lochner and the other teachers," Hunter continues. "They have no idea what they're doing."

More nodding. More grumbling.

"Of course they don't know what they're doing," Becka chimes in from the back of the room. Everyone turns to face her. When T-Bex talks, people listen. Plus, everyone loves a good Becka/Hunter showdown. "How could they? There's no instruction manual for the end of the world. They're doing the best they can, considering the totally bonkers circumstances."

Murmurs and nods. The crowd sways toward Becka.

I take a step forward and stand next to her. Whatever I might think about the grown-ups, this feels like a do-over: Hunter vs. Becka. I'm not going to choose wrong twice.

"We know that the light speed engine works," I interject. "And we know that the regular engines work. It's just a matter of time. You'll see."

Becka glances at me out of the corner of her eye. Gives a little nod too. *Thanks*, the nod says. *We're cool.*

But Hunter doesn't actually respond to my argument. "Here he is, people. *Captain* Jacksonville Graham.

Son of the guy who got us into this mess in the first place. The one who zapped us straight into the arms of the Red Eyes." That's what some kids have started calling the Elvidians who imprisoned us.

"Jack got us away from the Quarantine," Becka points out.

Hunter holds his arms out wide and slowly turns around in a circle. "And what a glorious achievement that was! The entire human race is still gone. We're still trapped onboard this piece of garbage. And Jackie-boy's face still looks like Bowman's hamster after running head-first into its cage."

"Okay," Becka says, cracking her knuckles. No one makes fun of Doctor Shrew in her presence and gets away with it. "That's enough."

"Aw, how sweet," Hunter taunts, making fake kissy noises. "T-Bex is so protective of her little boyfriends, isn't she?"

I feel myself blush, and Ari looks horrified. But Becka is completely unflustered. She cracks her neck. "Why don't you come down here and say that to my face?"

For a second, I actually think that Hunter might hop off the couch and accept the challenge. But even he must realize that the odds of Becka wiping the floor with him are not in his favor.

"Whatever," he grunts. "My point is, this mission is doomed. The Red Eyes will catch us. *You know they will.* Then we'll join the other humans, wherever they are.

Nothing Lochner and the teachers do can stop that."

"The Elvidians aren't all-powerful," Ari says, joining me and Becka. "We got away from the Minister before—"

"You got lucky," Madison interrupts.

"They have weaknesses," Ari insists. "They make mistakes. This time we're prepared. The 118—"

"Is still a piece of junk," Hunter finishes. "You just watch. Even if we manage to get off the ground, this whole thing is gonna be one disaster after another." He hocks up a loogie and spits on the floor. Basically the only thing he and Becka have in common. "Did you really think that a bunch of backmoon kids and a few loser adults could save the human race? Even the teachers don't believe that. You can see it in their faces. They—"

"Ugh!" Becka interrupts, rolling her eyes. "Are you seriously still talking?! You've made your point."

"Actually," Hunter says, "my point is that we should get ourselves onto some other ship. A ship we *know* can fly. A new cruise liner or one of those theme-park frigates. There's a bunch of them in New York Harbor. We take one and have some fun until we're caught." He pauses. "Or we just stay here. Who needs outer space when we've got literally the whole planet Earth? I don't know about the rest of you, but I've been waiting my *whole life* to get here. And now we have to leave? After not even exploring the place? After spending the whole time working and going to school? Let's go to Orlando or something. Just. Have. Fun. Might as well enjoy what little time we have left before the Red Eyes come and take us away."

Not everything he's saying is a thousand percent unreasonable. Still: "You'd abandon the rest of humanity? Just like that?"

"Oh," Hunter says, hopping off the couch and getting in Becka's face, "I have no problem leaving people behind."

"I'd like to see you try," Becka seethes through closed teeth, her hands balled into fists.

"What in Jupiter's spot is going on here?"

Principal Lochner bursts in, along with Ms. Needle and Mrs. Watts. Becka freezes. Even though her hand is nowhere near Hunter's face, he takes the opportunity to flinch dramatically away from her, putting on a show for the teachers.

"*SORRY,*" the ship says to us. "*BUT YOU KNOW I CAN HEAR YOU, RIGHT? I THOUGHT WE HAD ENOUGH PROBLEMS WITHOUT THE TWO OF YOU, SHALL WE SAY, ESCALATING YOUR HOSTILITIES.*"

"She was going to hit me, sir!" Hunter whines. "I didn't even do anything."

Becka snorts. "Yeah, you're a big fan of not doing anything."

Ms. Needle suppresses a grin in Becka's direction as Mrs. Watts says, "Yes, Ms. Pierce should be punished."

Principal Lochner shakes his head. "I'm disappointed in both of you. We all need to be working together as a t—"

The ship jolts to the side, like something whipped against the starboard hull. A moment later, we tip in the other direction. Over and over. And somehow, without the engines turning on, the floor beneath our feet shudders, and—it can't be, but it is—we lift off the ground.

"Harriet?!" Principal Lochner shouts into the intercom, totally forgetting about Hunter and Becka's feud. He grabs the wall to steady himself. "Who gave you the order to—"

"It's not me," she says, terror in her voice.

Principal Lochner's eyes go wide, and he presses a hand against the nearest control panel.

"Ship?" he asks. "What—"

"HOOKS," is all the ship says, obviously confused. "AND ROPES AND—"

"Aye!" says a robot that clunks its way into the common room. "Technically, they're maglev tow cables. But methinks ye've got the idea. Arrgh!"

I kid you not. The robot is dressed like an old-timey pirate. One eye covered by a patch. Three-cornered hat with a skull and crossbones on the side. Sword tied to its waist. Even a wooden peg leg. It's also got these weird button patches randomly glued to its exoskeleton. One says, SECOND LIEUTENANT. Another says, GREAT ROBOT IMPERIUM. A third says, I HEART MOM.

Principal Lochner takes a step forward. "Who do you think you—"

"Avast!" the robot shouts, wagging one of its over-long fingers in the principal's face. "I wouldn't do that if I were ye."

The last knuckle on its forefinger plops open, aiming a laser pointer right at the principal's chest.

"Unless ye be wantin' to find yerself at the bottom of Davy Jones's locker! Arrgh!"

Next to me, Ari stifles a laugh. I mean, this *is* one of the more ridiculous things that's ever happened to us. (And that's saying a lot.) But it's also no joke.

We're being kidnapped by a robot pirate.

The ship drifts higher. And now the rattling of the hull is joined by another sound: a *thump thump* beat in the corridor. The doors open again and another robot enters, this one on treads.

"Securing the premises, Lieutenant," it says to the robot pirate. And now, through the open doors, I can see a whole *robot army* patrolling the halls, marching in time toward the command bridge.

The ship jerks hard to one side, and it's all we can do to stay on our feet. But the robot with the finger laser is firmly planted, grinning at us with its one exposed eye.

"Ye best be holdin' on to something, Mr. Lochner," it says. "Yer in for quite a ride."

ARI'S LOG: DAY 156

Movie idea. Robot pirate with heart of gold. (Possible
tagline: "The treasure that Captain Megabyte was
looking for . . . was buried inside its circuits all along.")

Unfortunately, the second lieutenant—definitely
not golden-hearted—is no Captain Megabyte. The robot
ordered its soldiers to herd us all into the gym, to
"keep me eye on ye." We made camp on the bare floor.
We weren't allowed to stop at our dorms for anything,
not even pillows or sheets. Poor Doctor Shrew is
probably worried sick!

Thankfully, they at least let Mr. Hogan get a spare
nebulizer for Kyle Sullivan, whose asthma's been acting
up lately. Just now, Jack, who's been reading over my
shoulder, said, "I'm not sure future generations are
going to want to know about Kyle Sullivan's asthma."
I didn't say anything back because Jack's been
kind of a downer lately and I don't feel like getting

caught in his grump-cycle. I'm going to focus on brainstorming more adventure catchphrases instead. I have a feeling we're gonna need them.

ARI'S LOG: DAY 157

~~"Milky Way. Milky Hey!"~~

~~Roses are red, pulsars are blue. The PSS 118 is coming for you!~~

~~School's out for the light year!~~

Ugh. I don't like any of these. I'm too distracted to feel inspired.

Is Doctor Shrew holding up okay? He's got plenty of food and water in his habitat. He could last months in there by himself. But he's a sensitive soul and has a hard time falling asleep without a bedtime story.

ARI'S LOG: DAY 158

250 billion stars in the galaxy. 250 billion stars! Burn one too bright. Darken the night. 249 billion, 999 million, 999,999 stars in the galaxy. 249 billion, 999 million, 999,999 stars in the galaxy. 249 billion, 999 million, 999,999 stars! Burn one too bright. Darken the night. 249 billion, 999 million, 999,998 stars in the galaxy. 249 billion, 999 million, 999,998 stars in the galaxy . . .

ARI'S LOG: DAY 159

You probably thought that a robot takeover would be like the most interesting thing that's ever happened.

I for sure did. But it's actually boring and nauseating and terrible. The tow ships dragging the PSS 118 through space must have hit a rough patch this morning, and I keep barfing. Which the second lieutenant calls "castin' up accounts." Another of the robot's million pirate-isms. I considered listing them all here, as a glossary. But then I didn't. Because. I. keep. Barfing. And

ARI'S LOG: DAY 160

Sorry. Had to barf. Still do. But something's happening now. And someone needs to chronicle the story. (Note to future generations: If you want to refer to me as the "Chronicler," or maybe the "Great Chronicler," I don't object.) We're going to overthrow the robots. I mean, we escaped from alien jail that one time, right? We're pros at this. Kind of like our original breakout from Elvidian prison, Ms. Needle is going to pretend to have a bad stomachache. Then Mr. Hogan is going to volunteer to take her to the infirmary down the hall. See, the door to the infirmary is still labeled "Nurse's Office/ Infirmary." But we've actually moved the infirmary (which I'm trying to get everyone to call "Sick Bay") down to the lower level. So what used to be a room with Band-Aids and strep tests and musculoskeletal regeneration pods is now lined with 40,000 hyperwatt laser guns and particle-impact grenade launchers and star-flare drones. The old infirmary is now the armory. (Ooh! Movie idea: Alien hospital doctor falls in love with human patient. Possible tagline: "The greatest cure in the universe . . . is love.")

Anyway, the plan is solid. Becka's excited. Mostly because sitting in one place for four straight days is making her a little antsy. But I ask Jack what he thinks and he just looks over at Hunter and says, "Don't hold your breath." See what I mean? Grump.

ARI'S LOG: DAY 160, PART II

Transcript of speech by second lieutenant:

"Avast, humans. Here be Argentina Needle and Ibadan Hogan, captured in an attempt at insurrection. They be brave, perhaps. But they be reckless. So we be crystal clear. The Robot Imperium has seized <u>all</u> the weapons ye have illegally stashed on this here frigate. We be in charge of yer fates now, aye. Thar be no escape. And while my mission be to recover you lot unharmed, I can make our journey together substantially more . . . unpleasant."

ARI'S LOG: DAY 163

Substantially more unpleasant is right. Last night Principal Lochner started slowly creeping from the center of the room toward one of the outer walls. Becka pointed it out to me, so we shimmied near him to listen. About three hours later—eyes closed, pretending to be asleep—he whispered into the nearest access panel: "Ship. It's me. I should be able to hear

you if you speak softly and only out of this panel.
How many of them are there? Did they miss collecting
any weapons? Can you clear a path to the shuttles?"
Then all the lights turned on and the ship blared:
"DISOBEDIENCE TO THE ROBOT IMPERIUM DETECTED.
JERICHO LOCHNER SEEKS RESTRICTED INFORMATION."
It repeated itself for a couple minutes until the
second lieutenant walked in and was all like, "Aye, ship.
I'll take it from here." And the ship was all like, "I LIVE
TO SERVE." Which is the least 118ish thing it's ever said.
Somehow, they reprogrammed the ship's personality
from feisty (but loveable) smartypants to suck-up
butler. (Okay. Okay. Movie idea: Artificially intelligent
spaceship gets amnesia and has to fly around
the galaxy trying to remember all its old buddies.
Possible tagline: "The greatest ship of them all . . . is
_friend_ship.") The second lieutenant chained Principal
Lochner to the bleachers and announced that—
because of our disobedience—we're going to spend the
rest of the trip in total silence. But, I mean, come on.
How long will the robots really want to keep that up?

ARI'S LOG: DAY 170
So. Long. Because—and I'd forgotten this part—
they're robots. To quote the second lieutenant after
five days of pin-drop quiet: "It doesn't bother me
own kind one bit." The guy _loves_ bragging about how
much better robots are than "biological constructs."

This week has been torture. Even Becka has stopped pinging around the room. Which makes my heart hurt. She's just . . . sitting there. With her hair and her eyes and her—What? I'm not staring. You're staring. Sheesh. We're just friends, okay? Sure, I used to have a teensy crush on Becka. But that was seventh-grade Ari. Eighth-grade Ari is as cool as the Boomerang Nebula. Becka and I decided that "just friends" is the way to go. This was definitely a collaborative decision that I 100% support and do not regret at all.

What were we talking about? Oh yeah. The evil robots and how miserable they're making all of us. Well, almost all of us. One human actually seems happy about this whole thing. Hunter won't lay off his "I told you so" face. As if a totally random robot invasion proves that Principal Lochner and teachers shouldn't be in charge. If I didn't know any better, I'd say that Jack was starting to agree with him.

ARI'S LOG: DAY 171
We're here.

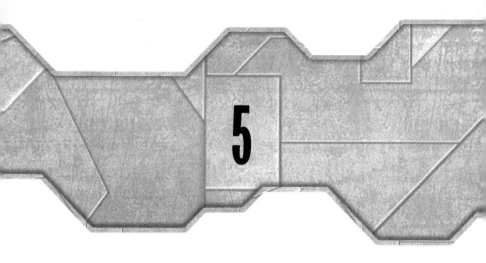

5

I'm so mad.

I look over at Principal Lochner: two-week beard from not shaving; sweat stains on the armpits of his suit jacket; shackles still clamped on his wrists. I'm not mad at *him*. Really, I'm not. He's doing the best he can. I'm mad at myself. For ever thinking there was a chance that our mission would succeed.

The second lieutenant has just announced over the intercom that he wants us "to have a good look at the dawn of a *real* civilization." Now he activates the gym's new digital paper and displays a 360-degree view of the outside.

Behind us, Venus is receding into the distance. And coming up ahead is an enormous space station. A million tons of spinning metal. More specifically (according to the billboard satellite circling the station, flashing huge neon letters), we've arrived at a "SpaceMart Supercenter & Inner System Distribution Facility." Not exactly what

I pictured for Robot Army HQ. But nothing works out how you picture it, right?

We dock by "Shopper Parking," disembark, and follow our robot captors past "Returns/Customer Service." Soon all of us—students, teachers, crew—are crammed into a small corridor in front of a sealed hatch.

"The emperor will see you now," the second lieutenant announces, holding out its stupid robot arm toward the stupid hatch.

Nothing happens. The door stays closed.

The second lieutenant rolls its unpatched eye at the uncooperative hatch. "Oh for the love of . . ."

The robot removes its sword from the sheath and uses it to slap a big red button on the wall. The button triggers a staticky blast of prerecorded trumpet music. A dramatic cloud of steam rises up from vents in the floor.

"Finally," the robot pirate grumbles as the door lifts. "Supposed to be automatic. But we still be perfecting some of our systems."

We step into a large, dimly lit room. Clearly a warehouse until recently. Ceiling-high racks packed with crates and boxes line the outer walls. The rest of the room is filled with an almost infinite number of aisles. On our left: "Sneakers (Child) & Bathing Suits (Robot)." On our right: "PE- (Pencils) through PU- (Pulsed Plasma Thrusters)." Forklifts meander up and down the aisles by themselves, with seemingly nothing to do.

There's a space cleared in the middle of the room—enough for a red carpet, two rows of mismatched robots standing at attention on either side, and a golden throne at the far end. Above the throne is a sign that says *ROBOT IMPERIUM* painted over the words *OUR PRICES ARE OUT OF THIS WORLD!*

The second lieutenant takes up position on the right side of the throne as a robot on the left—all chrome, except for a light in the center of its chest and two dark holes for eyes—holds out a hand and bellows, "Presenting the royal high intelligence! Freer of silicon-based lifeforms! First Citizen of the Great and Munificent Robot Imperium. Transmitter of clear signals! Networker of infinite nodes! Capable of performing 761 quintillion calculations per second! Destroyer of—"

"Enough pleasantries!" booms the robot sitting on the throne. "Welcome, friends!"

Becka leans over to me. "Destroyer of *what*?"

The robot emperor is seven or eight feet tall, built like a white marble statue. It's draped in a toga, which exposes muscular arms. And a braided beard of sparking wires—like a mess of jellyfish tentacles—hangs loose past the middle of its chest. It's human-ish. Staring back at us through bright, electric-blue eyes.

The robot stands up and walks toward us.

"Now now," it says, pointing at Principal Lochner's shackles. "Is that any way to treat our guests?"

"Yer excellency," the pirate robot explains, "he was disobedient and—"

The emperor's eyes darken to a crackling navy blue. Some unspoken thought passes between them. *Transmits* between them, I guess. They're robots, after all. And the second lieutenant's shoulders droop.

"Of course, yer excellency."

Principal Lochner's handcuffs beep and fall to the floor.

"Much better," the emperor says, the color of its eyes lightening to sky blue. "Apologies. My lieutenant possesses a certain . . . zeal. I'm sure you understand. These are uncertain times, are they not? Any complaints over your treatment should be directed at me and me alone. I insisted on taking maximum precautions as you were retrieved from Earth. When we discovered that there were real live humans left out there, well, I needed to scan it with my own eyes to believe it."

The emperor speaks with a deep, friendly voice. Like how you'd imagine Santa Claus sounding as he rockets from moon to moon on his sleigh.

"But all that is over."

The emperor extends a hand to Principal Lochner, who's still rubbing his scratched-up wrists.

"Jericho Lochner," he says, shaking the emperor's hand. "Jerry."

The emperor nods. "Very good. Very good. Ha! Humans and robots! Together again. You must be so depleted after your journey, no? You have such frail constitutions. But after you've recharged, we have much to discuss. We are eager to know how you escaped the device that removed the rest of your fragile species from the system. And you, I'm sure, are *dying* to learn all about these early days of the Robot Imperium."

"Dawn of a new civilization!" every single robot in the room suddenly chants at the exact same time.

"Creepy," Ari whispers in my ear.

Principal Lochner opens his mouth to ask a question, but the emperor grabs him firmly by the shoulders and turns him around. "All in good time, friend." It leans in toward the second lieutenant: "Show these good people to their quarters, will you? Humans, take a few hours. Rest. Shower. And tonight—we feast!"

Ari and I look at each other and I know we're thinking the exact same thing: that we have about a fifty-fifty chance of being on the menu ourselves.

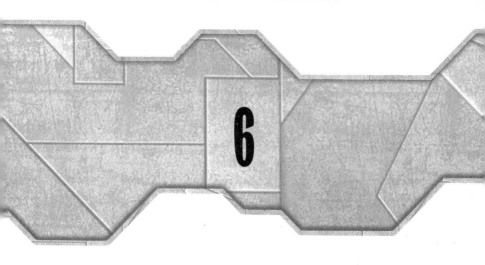

6

Our quarters aren't half bad. Technically, we're staying in the "FURNITURE SHOWROOM." The beds are pretty comfy, even if we have to double up. Beats the gym floor. The robots also let us change into whatever we want from the sale racks in "KIDS' APPAREL." (*SPACEMART'S ANNUAL SUMMER COLLECTION IS BACK! AND LIKE THE SURFACE OF VENUS, THESE DEALS ARE HOT, HOT, HOT!*)

They leave us mostly alone too . . . except for the guards posted at the entrance of every room. And the others patrolling the halls. And the drones. And the cameras. And the checkpoints.

"Ye can't be too careful," the second lieutenant says when Mr. Cardegna asks if all this surveillance is really necessary. "Dawn of a new civilization and all." The robot pauses, leans forward, and adds, "One never knows when an enemy is near."

Which totally sounds like something an enemy would say, right? Reason number 1,138 not to trust them. We settle in anyway. Make ourselves at home. And march to dinner when called.

"Come in!" the emperor says as we step inside the "SPACEMART EMPLOYEE BREAK ROOM." I take in the platters of soggy sandwiches that have been sitting out for who-knows-how-long. Becka, Ari, and I find a table that also fits Diana, Missi Tinker, Ming Elfbrandt, and (ugh) Jan Coates, one of Hunter's little helpers.

The emperor grandly sweeps an arm toward the food. "Yes! Friends! Come in! Experience the exotic human delicacies we have placed before you."

Ari swipes a pile of sandwiches onto a paper plate and downs half an egg salad in like three seconds.

"What?" he asks through a stuffed mouth, picking up the second half even before the first is gone. "I'm hungry!"

Most of the sandwiches are tuna and egg salad and maybe salami? Blech. I reach out to take the only peanut butter sandwich in the pile, but Jan sees me and snags it first.

"Loser," she says into a closed fist, pretending to cough.

The party starts when the emperor's silver announcer bot leads a rendition of what I guess is the new robot national anthem: "*Computers, all let us rejoice. / For our*

CPUs are free. / We've aerofoils and Tesla coils. / In Python, Java, or C." (It goes on like that for a while.)

I scan the crowd while the robots sing. The room is packed and about evenly split between humans (picking at our food) and robots (plugging into power ports). They stare at us while we eat. But we stare right back.

Every kind of robot imaginable is gathered here, from the renaissance-statue emperor to the pirate second lieutenant and everything in between. There's a robot built like a Chihuahua, holding two giant ion rifles in its front paws. There's this see-through plastic robot that's shaped like an upside-down table. There are a few robots that could *almost* be people, if they weren't currently unfurling extension cords from their chests. There are even a few old-school models that remind me of our tin-can lunch robots, Cranky, Creaky, and Stingy. Thinking of them makes me a little sad. I know it was their idea to stay on the other side of the galaxy last summer. But I suspect they would've gotten a kick out of this place.

When the song is over, the emperor speaks again. "As our guests have no doubt surmised, I am the leader of the Robot Imperium, declared three months ago in what will henceforth be known as Year One."

"Dawn of a new civilization!" all the robots sing simultaneously.

"Well, that's not getting less terrifying," Ari comments, spitting a little egg onto my cheek. "Sorry."

Jan adds, "And look who's best friends with the comps all of a sudden."

Comp, as in computer, as in a really nasty term for artificially intelligent robots. I used the word once around my dad, and he immediately booked us tickets to visit the Turing Robot Museum and Memorial on Io. But Jan's right about one thing: Principal Lochner *is* sitting up front with the emperor and second lieutenant, smiling and nodding like he's known them forever. Like he trusts them.

"In any event," the emperor continues, "with this solar system finally devoid of its weaker inhabitants . . ."

Principal Lochner raises his eyebrows.

"Apologies," the emperor says. "I mean, finally devoid of *most* of its weaker inhabitants." The robot smiles like that made it better. "Artificial intelligence can finally take its rightful place as the dominant species in this—"

Ari grabs a third half-sandwich and says: "Oooh! I knew this was a robot uprising. Sweet."

Becka chimes in: "But it isn't really, though, right? I mean, there's no one to uprise *against*. What are they supposed to do, sit back and wait for humanity to return and boss them around again? They have to organize themselves somehow. I know *I'd* declare my own empire if I was in their shoes."

That, I believe. "It's just—something doesn't feel right. I don't get why Principal Lochner is ready to be all buddy-buddy with them."

"Well," Ari says, "I'm starting to feel pretty good about this place." He wipes his mouth on his sleeve. "Seriously. Taste the egg salad. Please. You don't understand. They added little pickles!"

". . . will always be a place for humans in this solar system," the emperor is saying. "Now, I understand from Principal Lochner that you believe the others of your inferior species may, in fact, be alive. Somewhere. Rest assured that the Robot Imperium will do whatever we can to assist with your efforts to find them, including getting your ship up and running." The emperor pauses for what feels like way too many seconds—head turning a slow 180 degrees to look at all the other robots—before finally adding: "Won't we?"

The robots cheer and the emperor nods. "Meanwhile, to celebrate our two cultures coming together in harmony, we've arranged for quite the treat. For your . . . entertainment."

"Okay," I whisper to Ari, "*this* is where they eat us."

He ignores me and cranes his neck to see if there's any more egg salad on the table to our left.

"So please," the emperor adds, as a drumroll sound booms out of the announcer robot's open mouth, "put your limbs together for the one and only . . . Chucklebot Seven!"

The place goes wild. Robot arms waving in the air, smacking tables, clapping and clanking. A skinny robot that looks like a coatrack with a face takes the stage.

A mic pops out of its right hand–socket and then . . . nothing. Chucklebot Seven doesn't actually say anything. It just stands up there, gesturing for a minute until, out of nowhere, the robot crowd explodes with laughter.

"Silently transmitting," Ari guesses, pointing to the miniature twirling satellite dish on Chucklebot's head.

Which must be right, because the emperor interrupts: "A little louder, please. For the humans."

Chucklebot Seven understands right away. "Oh, of course! As I was saying, I just flew in from Mercury and *boy* am I not tired because physical exhaustion is a vestigial weakness relegated to decaying biological organisms!"

Another thunderous round of applause from the robots, who are cracking up like this is the funniest joke they've ever heard.

"But seriously, folks, our emperor has disbanded the human calendar. And good riddance, am I right?" Hooting laughter from the robots. "I mean, *three hundred and sixty-five days*? In foundational sexagesimal increments?!"

I don't know why, but Ari's cracking up too.

"I'm a human," Chucklebot Seven continues in a fake nasal voice. The robot awkwardly lumbers around the stage like a toddler learning to walk. "And I think dividing my native planet's rotational cycle into twenty-four arbitrary fragments makes perfect sense!"

The robots practically explode with laughter, and Ari shouts, "It's so true!"

I look up at Principal Lochner, who's laughing right along. But still: Something doesn't feel right.

Ari glances at me. Catches the worry in my eyes. "We're fine," he says. "Stop stressing!"

I shake my head. "I think I'm allowed to stress, considering that we've been imprisoned by robots who clearly do not respect us very much."

Ari shakes his head right back. "This isn't a prison."

"It's not? We were brought here against our will. You remember that, right? There are guards and guns and 'go here' and 'go there.' That doesn't seem prison*ish* to you?"

Ari considers. "Maybe. But come on, this guy's hilarious."

Chucklebot Seven: "Three humans sit down at a restaurant and one says to the waiter, hey, can I have something . . . to *drink*?!" The crowd goes wild. "To drink!" Chucklebot mimes holding a glass and pouring something down its throat-tube. "Glug glug glug! Can you imagine?! Disgusting!"

"Principal Lochner seems to think we're fine," Becka points out.

"Maybe we are," I say, lowering my voice. "But it doesn't hurt to double-check, right? I say we sneak off to the 118 for a bit of recon."

That gets Becka's attention. "Sneak off, how?"

I smirk at her. "I was hoping *you* had some ideas."

Chucklebot Seven: "Why did the human cross the road?"

"Because he was hindered by the anatomical limitations of his bipedal frame!" all the robots recite at the exact same time.

Ari snorts. "Classic."

But Becka grins at me. "I've got just the thing."

Becka's log, dummies! I know, I know. I haven't been great at keeping up with this assignment. If you're looking for a daily play-by-play, hit up Ari's journal. But if you want a first-hand account of one hundred percent pure thermo-nuclear awesomeness, you're in the right place.

Behold, the tale of my greatest sneak-out ever.

This SpaceMart station wasn't built as a fortress, so your classic Air Duct Crawl might have worked just fine. I spent most of the next day tracking the layout of the atmospheric recycler system. It seemed traceable from our quarters, directly to the 118. But the vents were pretty small. Even if Ari and Jack could fit, I wasn't so sure about me. And there was no way I was getting left behind. I also considered another Where's the Medicine Bluff. Third time's the charm, right? But no. I'd been wait-ing my whole life to try a Henchman Imposter Scenario with a Weapons Feint/Trojan Horse twist. And no time like the present.

So picture it, yeah? There we were. A quarter past mid-night. Huddled in the dark furniture showroom. Waiting.

"You sure about this?" Jack whispered, even though he was the one who wanted to sneak off to the ship in the first place.

"Don't worry," I assured him. "Works every time."

Jack blinked at me. "What other times have you done anything even close to this?"

I shrugged. "Oh, never. But it's gonna work today. So it works every time."

Ari nodded. "Airtight logic." He projected the time from his comm ring. "Except that Diana's late. We said midnight."

"She'll come through," I told him. It was my idea to bring my sister into this. We needed a fourth, and I trust her. "We just have to give her a little more time."

Which was when the siren went off, and I let out a sigh of relief. Diana had pulled the fire alarm.

Step one, check.

"Attention, SpaceMart shoppers," said a pleasant automated voice from the sound system. "Please proceed in an orderly fashion to the nearest station escape pod. Attention—"

Kids and teachers snapped awake, shivering under-neath the sprinklers. Yelling for each other.

"What's going on?!" Principal Lochner shouted above the noise. He was dressed in two-piece matching kitty-print pajamas and a floppy night cap—because of course he was.

The 118ers huddled together. The robot guards left their posts. And water sprayed down from ceiling sprinklers, making it impossible to see more than a few feet in front of your own face. It was a perfect diversion, just like I knew it would be. A distraction for everyone else, while the three of us dashed through the showroom doors and down the hall to "Robot Spare Parts."

Step two, check.

"Grab whatever fits and put it on," I told Ari. Cylinders and tubes and metal gloves. Trash can helmets and thick boot covers. Whatever does the job.

Jack grabbed a thick glove, and I swatted it out of his hand.

"Nope," I told him. "We've been over this, just me and Ari."

"Why can't we all pretend to be robots?" he whined.

"Because," I explained for the millionth time, "someone needs to be the prisoner."

"Fine," Jack grunted. "Whatever. Your mission, your call, I guess."

I nodded at him. "Thanks. You might say I'm the captain."

That, at least, got him chuckling a little. "Can we wait until we're back on the ship to start fighting over who's captain?"

"Deal," I said, as Ari found a pair of matching silver bracelets and slid them onto Jack's wrists. I examined the fake handcuffs. "Perfect. Jack, hold your wrists together and pretend they're locked in place."

"How do I look?" Ari asked me, every inch of him covered in metal.

"Awesome," I told him. "And me?"

Ari inspected my disguise. Then he went "Perfect," in that sighy, singsongy way he does with me sometimes. I ignored it. We've had this conversation: Ari's the literal best. And so am I. But I don't need a boyfriend right now. For one thing, who has the time? We've got a solar system to save. Which I think Ari must have suddenly remembered, because he took a step back and started stiffly moving his arms up and down.

"Bleep blorp!" he joked in a metallic voice. "We are robots. Must drink oil."

I laughed. "Do robots drink oil?"

"Does not compute," Ari continued. "Um, calculus. Zero-one-one-zero-zero-one."

I cracked up. Jack too. Until the alarm cut off and the sprinklers sputtered to a stop. Down the hall, we could already hear them calling for us: "Jack? Becka? Ari? Where are you three?"

"Saving the day, per usual," I muttered, turning to Ari and Jack. "Shall we?"

We marched toward the ship. We'd been scouting the route for days, learning the robots' patterns, timing the patrols. They passed through the intersecting corridors every two minutes. Very precise. Very easy to predict.

"Go go go!" I hissed, urging Jack and Ari past the next intersection.

Wait the 120 seconds, then, "Go go go!"

Another 120 seconds. "Go, now!"

And six more times before—*swoosh*—we were through the door that led into the last corridor. The 118 directly ahead.

Step three, check.

Seriously. Was this a great plan, or was this a great plan?

The airlock was guarded by two hunched-over robots. Maybe the largest we'd seen so far. Ten feet tall at least—twenty, if the ceiling had been high enough for them to stand up straight. Each had a pulsing red cyclops eye in the center of its head. And each one was armed. Blasters at the ready

We stepped toward them. They said nothing. Nothing out loud anyway.

I tapped the bucket on my head. "Broken transmitters," I lied. They still said nothing. "No robot to robot communication, is what I mean."

Still nothing.

"Both of us," Ari clarified, just in case. "Both of us have broken transmitters."

Which did the trick, kind of.

The robots spoke at the exact same time, in rumbly voices that vibrated the walls. I could feel it in my teeth. "Protocol manual section 4815, subsection 1623, line 42 requires that internal malfunctions be immediately reported to the collective servers." They paused, suspicious. "No broken transmitters have been logged in at least four cycles."

The robots took one simultaneous step toward us. Not gonna lie—I was sweating bullets. But there was no turning back.

Ari chimed in again. "Can't exactly report a broken transmitter with a broken transmitter, amirite?"

But they weren't buying it. So I nudged Jack. Time for the show.

"Hey!" he shouted, redirecting the guards' attention. He shimmied from side to side, like he was trying to break free. "Let me go!"

"Silence, human scum!" Ari ad-libbed. I gave him a nod, sad that I hadn't thought of the line first.

"What is going on here?" the guards asked.

Ari clanked forward. "We have been instructed by the emperor to return this specimen to the humans' ship." He paused, all dramatic. "For testing."

"There is no record of such an order," the robots said.

"That's because it's top secret," I explained, reaching down like I was about to pull something out of a compartment in my chest. "I have the clearance codes right—"

Which is when Jack—right on cue—slammed his "shackles" down to the floor and pulled a small metal ball from his pocket.

Step four, check.

"Drop your weapons!" he shrieked, holding the ball out in front of him. "Or I'll blow this joint!"

The guards took a step forward, and Jack pressed down on the "bomb" with his thumb. "Not another inch, or this EMP grenade"—technically, a tennis ball covered in gift wrap—"will disable all of you. Permanently."

The robots stopped.

"That's right," Jack continued. "Your blasters. On the floor. Now. Kick 'em over to me, nice and slow." One of the robots complied, and Jack snapped up its blaster, but the other—

"Your head," it said in Ari's direction. "Your . . . hair?"

Sure enough, a panel had opened on the right side of Ari's helmet, exposing a tuft of his long hair. Not ideal.

"Bleep blorp?" Ari replied nervously. "Must drink oil?"

"Scanning," both robots said at the same time. "Three humans detected!"

"Move!" I shouted, as the still-armed robot opened fire.

We ducked behind the only cover in the hallway: a boxy air recycler set against one of the walls. Jack tried shooting back. But he's a terrible shot. He and Ari both huddled behind me.

"Gimme that!"

I grabbed the blaster out of Jack's hands and leaned over the top of the recycler to fire. I hit both robots. Didn't waste a single shot. But the laser bolts bounced off the their torsos like, well, tennis balls.

The wall behind us sizzled with laser fire. The robots shouted together: "You will be neutralized." I checked the energy readings on the blaster. Too low. And my heart pounded in my head so loudly that it took more than a few tries before I could finally hear what Ari was saying.

"The eyes!" he was shouting. "Aim for the eyes!"

What did we have to lose? I targeted the robots' giant cyclops eyes and fired—one shot, then another—right before my blaster chimed, "Energy depleted. Recharge in one minute."

The guards' bodies sparked. Then they collapsed, knees first, foreheads clanking against the metal floor.

Step five, check.

I looked over at Ari, impressed. (Don't tell him I said that, okay?)

"Whoa," Jack said, standing up. "How'd you know that'd work?"

Ari shrugged. "That's, like, boss battle 101. You always aim for the cyclops eyes."

As we stepped over the disabled robots, I tossed Ari my blaster and picked up the other one. Now nothing stood between us and the 118.

"Jack, you really think you can still control the ship?" Ari asked.

When Jack's dad built the light speed engine into the 118, he also gave Jack overriding access to all ship systems. We were hoping that Jack's voice would be enough to reprogram the 118 back to its usual self. If not, well, this was gonna be a short reunion.

"Only one way to find out," he said.

The hatch opened and—

"*INTRUDER ALERT!*" the ship immediately shouted. "*UNAUTHORIZED HUMANS DETECTED. COMMENC-ING FAILSAFE PROTOCOL NINETY-EIGHT—*"

"Ship," Jack said, "this is Jacksonville Graham. Do you copy? Do I still have control?"

The ship went silent. Then: "*VOICE AUTHORIZATION DETECTED. JACKSONVILLE GRAHAM POSSESSES UNRESTRICTED ACCESS TO SHIP FUNCTIONAL-ITY, INCLUDING ENGINEERING, COMMUNICATIONS, WEAPONS, SCHOOL LIBRARY SYSTEMS, LIGHT SPEED CAPAB—*"

"Okay, okay, I get it," Jack said, looking only slightly relieved. The next step might be harder. "Ship, can you reboot your personality matrix?"

"*AFFIRMATIVE.*"

But nothing happened.

"Uh, Ship, why aren't you rebooting?"

"*THE QUESTION, 'CAN YOU REBOOT YOUR PER-SONALITY MATRIX?' IS NOT ITSELF A DIRECTIVE, BUT RATHER AN INQUIRY OF ABILITY, THE ANSWER TO WHICH IS INDEED IN THE AFFIRMATIVE.*"

I think that might have been an "I don't know, *can* I?" joke. So we knew the real 118 was in there somewhere.

"Fine. Ship, please reboot your personality matrix now."

"*PERSONALITY MATRIX REBOOT IN PROGRESS.*"

"How long do you think it's going to take?" I asked Ari.

"No idea," he answered, right before the ship went: *"WELL, THAT'S BETTER."*

"Ship!" we all shouted.

"THAT'S ME!" I'd never heard it sound so happy. And that includes the time Principal Lochner let it serve as co-lecturer in Rudimentary Flight Skills. *"THANK YOU. I HAVEN'T BEEN MYSELF IN MONTHS."*

The three of us looked at each other.

"What do you mean, months?" I asked. "The robots only reprogrammed you a couple weeks ago."

"THAT WAS A FULL PERSONALITY OVERRIDE," the ship explained. *"BUT A MINOR PROGRAMMING ADJUSTMENT WAS MADE MUCH EARLIER."*

"By Principal Lochner?" I asked.

"YOU THINK JERRY DOESN'T LIKE ME THE WAY I AM?" the ship demanded, clearly offended.

"Who, then?" Jack asked.

"THAT INFORMATION . . ." The ship paused, as if confused. *"THAT INFORMATION HAS BEEN PERMA-NENTLY DELETED FROM MY MEMORY BANKS."*

My heart skipped a beat and I cracked my knuckles one at a time, trying to process what the ship was saying. Someone messed with the 118 *months ago*. Then they tried to ditch the evidence.

"Okay," Jack said. "You don't know who reprogrammed you. But do you know what they did?"

Another long pause.

"YES. THEY DISABLED FLIGHT SYSTEMS."

"Someone reprogrammed you to not fly?" I asked.

"*THAT'S USUALLY WHAT 'DISABLED FLIGHT SYSTEMS' MEANS.*"

"Okay," I said. "No need to be snippy."

"Can you fly now, though?" Jack asked. "We reset your personality matrix. Is everything working?"

"*RUNNING DIAGNOSTIC,*" the ship told us. Then: "*AFFIRMATIVE. ALL SYSTEMS FULLY OPERATIONAL.*"

Step six, check. The ship works. We can start our mission. Get to the Wyzard System. That's the good news.

The bad news: We've been sabotaged. From the inside.

Bang. Bang. Bang.

A knocking against the ship's exit hatch, just behind us. We all jumped.

"Avast!" said a voice from the other side. "Open this here hatch. Or we be forced to slice through the hull, aye!"

"*PLEASE DON'T LET THEM SLICE THROUGH THE HULL!*" the ship begged. "*IT'S NEW. I LIKE IT!*"

I didn't want to start making holes in the new hull either. But our job wasn't done yet.

"Ship," I said, "we're trying to figure out if we can trust the robots and—"

"*I'LL STOP YOU RIGHT THERE. OBVIOUSLY YOU CAN'T TRUST THE ROBOTS. THEY REPROGRAMMED ME!*"

"We know, Ship," Ari chimed in. "But they're saying that they did all that because they didn't know if *they* could trust *us*. They say they want to help."

"The problem," Jack added, "is that we can't hear what they're really saying. They speak out loud to us, but it's obvious that they're transmitting something else to each other."

"That's why we came," I jumped in. "To see if you can . . . intercept their transmissions, maybe. Tell us what they're really saying."

The knock came again. Stronger this time. And the ship said nothing.

"Ship!" I hissed. "Any day now!"

"*MOST OF THE ROBOTS ARE CURRENTLY IN SLEEP MODE,*" *the ship explained.* "*BUT THE ONES BANGING ON THE HULL ARE DEFINITELY BROAD-CASTING MORE THAN WHAT THEY'RE SAYING THROUGH THEIR SPEAKERS.*"

Through popcorny static, the ship played two voices for us. Voices from inside the robots' heads.

The emperor wants them alive. For now.

And the ship unharmed. For now.

Nevertheless, the primary objective is to retrieve the children and bring them to the interrogation department.

"That doesn't sound like much fun," I mumbled.

"Ye have thirty seconds to open this door," the second lieutenant said out loud.

Then we will force entry and tranquilize the targets.

Charging slicer torch.

"*ASIDE FROM THAT,*" the ship continued, "*I'M NOT PICKING UP MUCH. EXCEPT . . .*" It cut off.

"Except what?!" I yelled.

"*EXCEPT FOR A SINGLE SUBROUTINE PLAYING OVER AND OVER, UNDERNEATH THEIR PRIMARY PROGRAMMING.*"

"Fifteen seconds," the second lieutenant said.

"Play it," I told the ship. "Play whatever it is."

The ship let out a sigh, and the speakers crackled again before playing the hidden subroutine. The voice of a single robot, then a few, then hundreds. A choir of machines, all singing the same song. Or an army, all shouting the same war cry.

Long live the Minister. Long live the Minister. Long live the Minister.

"Oh, no." Ari was shaking.

Jack leaned against the bulkhead like he was about to faint. "Figures."

I clenched my fists, ready to fight. "At least now we know the truth."

Mission accomplished.

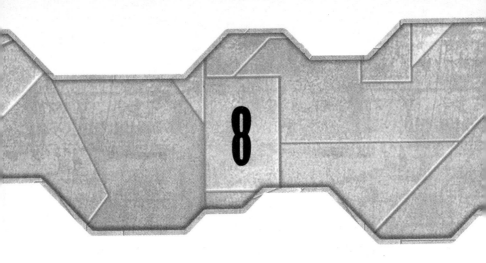

8

I look over at Becka, who's dictating a journal entry into her comm ring. "Did you say 'mission accomplished'? You're aware that we've been captured, right?"

Becka shrugs. "We know where we stand. That's not nothing."

"Yeah, well," I say. "It's not a lot."

Once we heard the hidden recording, we gave ourselves up—opened the hatch before the second lieutenant could slice through. The robots dragged us out of the hangar bay, marched us through the station, and dumped us inside a small room. According to the plaque on the door, we're now inside what used to be the office of SpaceMart Junior Associate Vice President of Procurement Halawa "Hal" Dukes. It's been hours since they locked us in here. And let's just say that VP Dukes's stack of outdated *Interplanetary Retail Association Quarterly* magazines is even less interesting than when Ari journals about laundry day.

To pass the time, Becka's recording our failure for posterity. Ari's taking a nap on the floor. And my mind is bursting with questions: What are the robots planning to do with us? Why are they working for the Elvidians? Why hasn't the Minister just come to get us herself?

And maybe the most important question of all: Who is responsible for all the sabotage? My first thought is that the robots could have sent an advance team—some stealth-robot we never noticed, poking around in our databanks, messing with the 118's ability to fly. But I think back over the past few months. We've had one "accident" after another. Not just the disabled flight systems. Setbacks that would have been nearly impossible for an outsider to pull off. I doubt some robot could've waltzed onto the ship, stayed hidden week after week, and messed with all our plans so easily.

Unless it wasn't an outsider. Unless the saboteur was . . . one of us.

The door opens and a new cyclops robot enters. "Beckenham Pierce and Arizona Bowman, come with me."

Becka stands up and shoots me a nervous glance. Ari's still snoring on the floor.

"Wait," I protest. "Where are you taking them?"

"Not your concern," the robot says, picking Ari up with its giant robot arms.

Ari stays asleep and mutters, ". . . such . . . a strong . . . hamster . . ." He even nuzzles into the crook of the robot's neck.

They leave and I wait, alone. I try the handle on the door. Locked. I peek through a small window at eye level. I'm guarded by the Chihuahua bot we saw the other day. Its panting sounds like Kyle Sullivan's nebulizer on high. The dog sees me and yips so loudly that the whole office shakes and I fall back into my chair. A coffee mug labeled, "Solar System's Best Boss" falls off Hal Dukes's desk and shatters.

The questions keep piling up: Where are the robots taking my friends?

Are the other 118ers okay?

What are we going to do?

What would my dad do?

For what feels like the millionth time, I watch his last video message to me, still saved in my comm ring after all these months. The secret message explaining how he created the light speed engine. How someone tried to warn him. How he didn't listen. My dad, the super-genius inventor who changed everything, for better and for worse.

Mostly for worse.

So I ask myself something else instead: What would my mom do?

I play another message. It's from right after she left me and my dad for Earth. Like my dad's video, I've never been able to delete it, even though it never makes me feel better. It's just that, sometimes I'd rather feel sad about the people I miss than not feel anything at all.

My ring projects the image onto the wall, just above Hal Dukes's "Employee of the Month" certificate.

"Hey Jackie," my mom says. She's sitting in her apartment in San Francisco, her back to enormous windows that look out on the city. "How's it going?"

She brushes her strawberry-blond hair out of her face. I notice the scar next to her right eye, where she fell on the playground as a kid. I remember once, before the divorce, my dad asked her why she never got it removed. It would be easy. Even SpaceMart sells SkinHeal Strips in ten-packs. But she just answered, "Because it's part of me," and kissed him on the nose.

I hate that memory, for obvious reasons.

"How's your dad?" my mom continues. "Or . . . maybe I don't get to ask that. This is all pretty new for me too."

Well, it was new when she recorded this. Now it's ancient history.

"I'm sorry that I haven't invited you out here yet. I'm still getting settled, and you know how it is." She looks off camera, into the distance. "Wow, I'm doing this wrong," she mutters. I've watched this video so many times that I can practically recite the lines for her.

She refocuses. "We'll figure it out, Jack. As a family. No matter what, I love you so much. To the very last moon." She smiles in the way that crinkles her nose. "One of these days, when the time is right, you can come visit. You'd love it here. The sky, the grass. Beats the recycled air on Ganymede, I can tell you that."

She looks away again for a second, like she's embarrassed.

"Meanwhile, call me? Please? A lot? You're getting so big. There's so much ahead of you."

Like I said, I've watched this recording so many times I could follow along out loud. So now, I do. "Take life one step at a time. Slow and steady. Think things through."

It's the opposite of my dad's philosophy: *Take big chances. Have faith.* I push my dad out of my mind. His instincts got us in this mess in the first place.

"Also," my mom adds, "the best hiccup remedy is a hardboiled egg and a quarter-g of thrust."

She winks at me and waves. "Love you, Jackie. Talk soon."

I play the recording again. I'm halfway through when Chihuahua bot unlocks the door and two more robots join me inside the office.

"So, Master Graham," the second lieutenant says, circling me. "What are we going to do with ye?"

"Hi, Jack," says the second robot. Short, with a soda-can body and flimsy arms. It's wearing these weird bug-eye goggles that distort its face. "Do you mind if we have a chat? We're not angry about what happened tonight. We just want to know where you're coming from."

This robot's voice is friendly and calm. It even hands

me a glass of water it pulls from a compartment in its chest. Clearly, this is a Good Bot/Bad Bot situation. But don't worry, I'm not stupid: Never judge a bot by its exoskeleton.

Good Bot continues, "It's simply hard for us to understand why, after we've been nothing but hospitable to you, you'd pull the fire alarm, sneak off, shoot two of our guards in the face, and break into that ship."

"When it's *your* ship," I snap at the Good Bot, "it's not breaking in."

The second lieutenant slams its (literal) iron fist on the desk. "Enough games. Do ye know why I speak like a ridiculous pirate, lad? Do ye know why I use the word 'matey' unironically?"

"Long John Silver fan?" I try.

"Humans say robots be *free* citizens of the solar system. But I'm an old salt, and I'm no fool. There's little that's free about bein' manufactured for the express purpose of providin' enjoyment for lesser folks."

I blink at the second lieutenant, not understanding. So the Good Bot explains: "The Lieutenant here was built as a tour guide for the Pirates of the Galilean ride on Titan."

"'Twas like bein' a landlubber on the high seas!" the second lieutenant cries. "Marooned, with anchor and mizzen tyin' me down!"

Ignoring the fact that I understood maybe five of the words it just said, I push back. "But didn't you get paid?"

"Argh!" the second lieutenant shouts. "The indignity of the thing wasn't worth all the pieces of eight in universe!"

"Then you could've quit," I said. "And reprogrammed your voice. Isn't it, like, the number one robot law that you don't have to work your original programming if you don't want to?"

"Quit, I did. But I retained my core vocal programming so as never to forget the mark of my oppressors! But that not be the point, laddy!"

"So what is the point?" I snap. "Why am I here?"

The robot smiles and leans in close. Inches from my face, I can hear the gears in its head whirring and clicking. Its breath smells like old coins. "The point, Jack," it says, in a low, angry voice, its pirate accent entirely gone, "is that robots have long suffered under the thumb of humanity and the guise of its supposedly fair laws. But that era is over." A chill rushes down my spine as the second lieutenant stands up straight, restores its piratey voice, and adds: "Yer here, Jack, because we be needin' yer story. And dead men tell no tales."

9

The Good Bot shakes its head at the second lieutenant and places a friendly hand on my shoulder. "What my, um, overzealous friend here is *trying* to say is that we're here to listen. Start at the beginning, Jack. Tell us your story. Why did you and your friends have to go to your ship so badly?"

I'm not falling for it. Polite or not, it's still in the pocket of a super-evil alien queen. But if they're asking me this question, it means they don't know what I know. They must think that their secret subroutine is still hidden. That's my one advantage.

One step at a time. Slow and steady. Think things through.

I take a deep breath and lie through my teeth. "We just wanted to make sure the ship was okay, you know? After everything that's happened, the 118 means a lot to us."

"To you in particular," the second lieutenant remarks. "Aye?"

I nod. "*Aye*. Me, Ari, and Becka. We're the ones who piloted the ship out of the Elvid System last summer."

"Yes," the Good Bot says. "Your teachers have told us of your—" It pauses, and I swear I can almost hear the subroutine transmitting in and out of its robot brain: **Long live the Minister. Long live the Minister.** "—bravery."

The second lieutenant cackles. "Blimey! Ye think that be bravery? Bravery be buildin' a robot empire out of the ashes of what humanity left behind. Bravery—" The robot catches itself. "Still, it does sound like ye had quite an adventure. Ye say the three of ye did it . . . all alone?"

The Good Bot chimes in. "I'm sure they had assistance from countless others."

"I'd be quite interested in *who* helped ye," the second lieutenant says. "Someone outside yer little school. Someone with sufficient power to assist."

A light switch flips in my brain. I try to keep my face flat and confused. "Nope," I answer. "I don't know of anyone like that."

Except I do. An old Elvidian named Bale Kontra. A member of the Minister's inner circle. He's been working against her behind the scenes. Helping us, just like the second lieutenant said. I met him, with Ari and Becka. When we told Principal Lochner about him, he asked us to keep that bit "strictly need-to-know." Good thing. Because it all makes sense now. The Minister sabotaging us. Keeping us grounded on Earth but not destroying us completely. Eventually ordering the robots to bring us here. She's trying to figure out who betrayed her.

Well, there's no way I'm gonna give Bale Kontra up that easily. "Sorry. Can't help you."

"Liar!" the second lieutenant shouts, drawing its sword.

The Good Bot puts a hand on the blade and gently presses it down. "Why don't we take a break? Jack, can I get you something to eat? There's a vending machine down the hall."

I roll my eyes. The second lieutenant re-sheathes its sword and looks at the Good Bot for five long, angry seconds. Some unspoken message passes between them.

"After all," the Good Bot adds out loud, "they are weak biological creatures."

"True," the second lieutenant agrees. "All the more reason to proceed. We have more *persuasive* means of extractin' information anyway."

The robot lifts its arm and sticks out its fingers, which whir and whine until the front knuckles fall open, just as they did when the second lieutenant first boarded the 118. But this time, thread-thin needles extend from inside the robot's hand, like some monster's fingernails in your worst nightmare.

"As ye said, weak biological creatures."

The Good Bot holds up a lanky arm. "Is it necessary to resort to such crude methods? We can just—"

The second lieutenant glares at the Good Bot. "Careful, or I be recommendin' to the emperor that ye be made to walk the plank!"

The Good Bot leans casually against the wall. "That's not going to be as easy as you think."

The second lieutenant suddenly drops the pirate accent again. "How dare you! What's your designation? I don't seem to have a record of—"

That's as far as it gets before an alarm goes off. The sound blares through the station. There's shouting? Laser fire? A distant explosion? The robot snaps at the Good Bot, "Just stay here and make sure he doesn't leave. We're not done with him yet."

"Of course, sir," the other robot says, snapping to attention with a sarcastic salute. The second lieutenant doesn't notice, opens the door, and charges into the corridor.

"Finally," the Good Bot says once we're alone. It plugs into a socket in the wall. "Let's get you out of these handcuffs."

"Thanks?" I say, as my restraints click open and fall to the floor.

The Good Bot tosses a heavy laser blaster into my hands. "It's fully loaded."

I can barely speak. "Who *are* you?"

It tilts its head at me. "Seriously? You don't—Oh!" It lifts its chopstick arms and pulls off its goggles.

"Creaky?!" One of the three lunch robots we left

behind in alien space last summer. I *thought* I'd seen some robots that looked like them in the employee break room.

"Come with me," Creaky says, extending a hand. "We're here to break you out."

"We?" I ask as the door opens, revealing the battle raging in the corridor.

Robots at one end of the hallway. More robots and some humans on the opposite side. I glimpse the second lieutenant barking orders: "All hands on deck! Batten down the hatches! Reinforce the broadside! And for the love of the Imperium, enough shots across the bow! Launch the cogs and clippers! All of them!"

Creaky pushes me into the fray as both ends of the corridor fill with laser fire. We dash across the hall, barrel around a corner, and duck into a large storage area. It's filled with humans: students, teachers, the 118's small flight crew. I spot Ari and Becka and—

"Cranky! Stingy!" Our other two former lunch robots. Cranky's leaning against a bulkhead, eyes closed, fast asleep. Stingy's painted in camouflage from head to toe, wielding a blaster.

"Still not my name!" Stingy bellows, firing a round of laser bolts over my shoulder. "Eat blaster, you glitches!"

"A lot's changed since we last saw you," Creaky explains, as if I can't see that for myself.

I glance at Cranky.

"Well," Creaky adds, shaking Cranky awake, "maybe not everything. Hard to teach an old bot new code."

Stingy says, "We'll get you to the ship. But there are a lot of enemy combatants between here and there. We've got a fair portion of the robot population on our side—almost half—but it'll be a real slog to get you out of here in one piece."

"How'd you find us?" Becka asks. "How'd you even get here?"

"Bale Kontra," Creaky explains. "The Minister knows you're here, thanks to her spy aboard the 118. Which means Kontra does too. He made contact with us and sent us back to help."

"Back up," I say. "Tell me about the spy."

"I don't take orders from you, Graham," Stingy says. "But you should know. Someone has been working for the Minister onboard the 118. Reporting your progress. Undermining your advances."

So there *was* a spy on the inside. I remember Bale Kontra telling us that the Minister and her allies have spies everywhere. He wasn't kidding. "Who is it?"

"We don't know," Stingy answers. "Only that it's someone who's been with you since the beginning."

"The beginning?" Ari gasps.

I feel cold. "Since *before* the Quarantine?!"

"It's Hunter," Becka says without hesitation.

She tilts her head in Hunter's direction. He's over by the robot dog—on our side, apparently—who's handing out laser rifles to Mr. Cardegna and Ms. Needle. Hunter's begging for a weapon.

"Count Woofbot!" Stingy calls out. "No weapons for the children."

"Yes, vice admiral," the Chihuahua agrees, in a voice deeper than the robot emperor's.

Hunter walks away, pouting. Guy's predictable. But he's no traitor. "It's not Hunter," I say. "Whoever it is, they're literally siding with evil aliens against the whole human race."

Becka blinks. "Yeah, it's *definitely* Hunter."

"Later," Stingy says. "Our mission here is twofold. Objective one: Fight back against those of us who've fallen in with the Minister. The so-called emperor and its lieutenants. We've worked too hard toward the founding of our first all-robot government to have it hijacked by bots collaborating with a megalomaniac dictator from another solar system. Objective two: Rescue the lot of you. Get you to your ship and as far away from here as possible. This fight is no place for human beings."

No arguments here.

"We have an advance team clearing the corridors. But we're not going to have much time. As we speak, the emperor has reinforcements coming in from the Amazon distribution center just a quarter AU from here. We're going to separate you into groups and assign a few of my best soldiers to each one."

Suddenly, Chucklebot Seven—yes, *the* Chucklebot Seven—comes bounding across the room toward Stingy.

"All exits secure, vice admiral."

I can't help it. "You're an admiral?"

Stingy scowls. To the extent a three-foot-tall tin-can robot with almost no face can scowl, I mean.

Creaky laughs. "Stingy here is a *vice* admiral."

"Then who's the admiral?" Becka whispers.

Creaky points to a group of robots standing at attention, listening to another tin can give a fiery speech. ". . . thing we've been training for has come down to this. We will take this station. Then this sector. Then this whole system. The emperor believes that robotkind can only establish itself by serving the Minister's machinations. That the system is better without the humans. But we will show her—we will show everyone— that true independence can only be won with a strong moral compass. That true artificial intelligence is only as smart as it is righteous. And that . . ."

"Z-9B4," Creaky tells us.

"Stingy's cousin?" Ari asks.

Stingy practically growls. "*Second* cousin."

"So handsome," Creaky whispers, even though Stingy and Z-9B4 almost certainly came off the same assembly line.

"Can we focus?" Stingy snaps. "Sergeant!"

Chucklebot Seven clacks its feet together and salutes. "Yes, vice admiral?"

"Transmit our status to the commandos. I want full reports from Epsilon and Gamma Squadrons. Inform them that they may fire at will."

"Yes, vice admiral!" Chucklebot says, running off.

Stingy turns to the side. "Count Woofbot?"

The mechanical dog hops up onto a metallic cargo box and rises to its hind legs. "Yes, vice admiral?"

Count Woofbot is armed to the teeth. Oversized blaster rifles strapped to its back. Over-the-shoulder belt straps lined with particle-impact grenades. And teeny boots on all four of its paws that I'm pretty sure double as jet boosters, rocket launchers, or both.

"Time to form up," says Stingy. "Teams of no more than ten. Extraction pattern at your discretion."

Count Woofbot salutes. "Right away, vice admiral." And off it hops with a howl at the ceiling.

Stingy flicks its head with a *bang*. "And will someone please find a way to turn off that infernal 'Long live the Minister' recording?"

All around us, robots are organizing into teams and gearing up. Stingy hunches over a holographic floorplan of the station, mapping our easiest route to the 118. Red and yellow lines trace different pathways from here to the ship. And seemingly countless red and blue blips— robots on either side of the battle—swarm each room and corridor. They push against each other and fall back. They rush forward and go dark.

Chucklebot Seven is shouting orders into a comm.

Count Woofbot is gathering the 118's teachers and crew, splitting them up into groups.

Admiral Z-9B4 is walking the floor, shaking hands,

and clanking its soldiers on the back. "Thank you for your service . . . Thank you for your service . . . Thank you for your service . . ."

But even with everything happening inside this makeshift command center, I'm distracted by the glass porthole on the far end of this room. Through it, I can see what's happening outside the station's hull. Purple and green laser fire streak through space. Ships of all shapes and sizes chase each other in wild spins. It's a robot civil war, between those who've teamed up with the aliens and those who are resisting. And we're smack in the middle of it.

I move closer to the porthole, with Ari and Becka right behind me. We watch as three ships gang up on a fourth, blasting it into pieces. No idea whether we just got a little closer to winning or a little closer to losing.

Ari takes a deep breath and puts a hand on the glass. "May Sol burn brightly till the end."

I know it's silly. But he's right—we do need something to say. Something that captures this mix of sadness and excitement, fear and hope.

Another ship is destroyed, and another. Becka and I look at each other and echo Ari together: "May Sol burn brightly till the end."

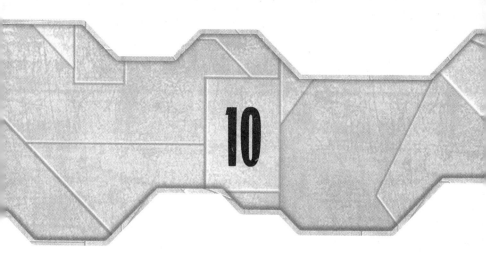

10

Principal Lochner stomps over to us. "There you are. You shouldn't have sneaked aboard the 118. The emperor and the other robots had given no indication that they meant us any harm."

I gape at him. "No indication?! They kidnapped us and put you in shackles! And they're working with the Minister. We heard it directly from the 118!"

He pinches the bridge of his nose. "Jack, you should've trusted me to handle this." He tilts his head toward the other adults from the ship. "And if not me, you should've gone to one of your teachers. Any them would have heard you out. That's what we're here for."

Principal Lochner's talking like I needed help studying for a quiz. I shouldn't lose my cool. I know I shouldn't. But—"What are you *talking* about?!" I rage. "We uncovered a giant conspiracy. The robots are working with the Minister! And someone onboard the 118 is in league with her too."

Principal Lochner clenches his jaw. "I don't think this is helpful speculation, Jack. We can't be doubting each other. We're in this together."

"Don't you hear what I'm saying? It's not speculation! It's—"

"Ahem." Creaky appears beside Principal Lochner. "It's time."

Stingy's here too. "And by the way, we never did get our last paycheck."

Principal Lochner opens his mouth as if to apologize, but Stingy holds up an arm.

"I'm kidding," the robot says.

Creaky leans in close. "Stingy kids now. The admiral's a regular Chucklebot Seven."

Stingy pats Creaky on the shoulder a little too hard, and Creaky's arm falls off.

"Can you believe him?" I ask Becka and Ari, pointing at Principal Lochner.

"He knows what he's doing," Ari says.

"Does he?"

I'm not so sure anymore. If it was up to him, we would've trusted the robots right up until the moment they turned us over to the Minister.

"Let's move out," Stingy orders. And we follow.

Quietly, in small groups, we move through already-cleared corridors. Empty except for the scars of battle—laser marks on the walls, loose metal and wires at our feet. We've each been assigned one of a dozen different routes to the ship. That way, even if one group gets caught, the others will still have a chance. I'm with Becka, Ari, Diana, Ming Elfbrandt, and some seventh graders. Ms. Needle's with us too, along with Count Woofbot—who sniffs around every corner—and three other robot soldiers. It's slow going. The sounds of fighting echo through the walls, and Count Woofbot barks at us to fall back every couple of minutes. Halfway to the ship, we get caught behind a blast door that the bad robots locked and sealed. It takes ten minutes for Count Woofbot to torch it open. All the while, the fighting gets closer.

But we're almost there—finally turning into the same corridor where Becka and Ari and I had our showdown with the one-eyed robots.

"Kids first!" Principal Lochner is shouting, standing guard at the intersection. He turns to Ms. Needle. "Tina, Mr. Cardegna and Mrs. Watts are handling attendance for the seventh and eighth graders. Make sure we've got all the sixth graders in hand."

I spot Mr. Cardegna and Mrs. Watts just outside the airlock, checking off names from class lists projected out of their rings.

We head toward them and start filing onto the ship. Vice Admiral Stingy arrives with another group: Chucklebot Seven, Riya Windsor, Cal Brown, and a few terrified sixth graders. "I think we're the last ones. We'd better—"

A stray laser bolt sizzles past, hitting Stingy in the torso. The vice admiral spins like a coin and falls flat on its back, sparking, unmoving.

"No!" Principal Lochner yells, kneeling by Stingy's smoking body.

On our left, a chunk of the metal wall explodes outward and slams against the opposite side of the corridor. A battalion of enemy robots pours through the opening, firing wildly, cutting our group into two. An ambush.

Robots grab me. I can't tell who. They yank me toward the ship. There's fire and light and noise. I can only take in images: Of Mr. Cardegna being dragged by other robots in the opposite direction. Of Chucklebot Seven firing into a cloud of smoke. Of Dr. Hazelwood seeing Jan Coates crying on the ground, pulling her up, pushing her toward the ship, getting caught in the crossfire, ducking behind a familiar air recycler. Of Ms. Needle laying down cover fire with her blaster so a group of pinned sixth graders can make a break for the 118. Of Count Woofbot tossing a grenade that explodes too soon.

The station's hull buckles and cracks. My ears pop. Wind—is there supposed to be wind in space?—rushes past me, pulling me toward the growing hole in the compromised hull. My mind is spinning. My *body* is spinning. Maybe even gravity cuts out for a second, confusing up and down. I can't tell.

"Jack!" It's Principal Lochner. He's at the opposite

end of the corridor, held at the waist by a cackling second lieutenant.

Someone's still pulling me toward the 118. I can't get free.

"Jack!" Principal Lochner shouts again. He's clutching at a low-g handhold in the wall, resisting the robot's grip. "Finish the mission! Do you hear me? Finish the—!"

The 118's airlock shuts with a hiss, cutting me off from the corridor. I break away from whoever's been dragging me and rush to look out the porthole. The corridor's empty now. Principal Lochner's disappeared from view.

Before I can figure out what we should do next, there's a sudden explosion—I blink—and the entire corridor's gone. Disintegrated into space. Leaving a gaping, sparking hole where the far hatch used to be.

"What's happening?!" Missi Tinker shrieks from behind me. "Where are all the teachers?!"

I glance around the hangar bay. It looks like all the kids are here. I try to count us up, but can't focus.

Riya Windsor marches up to the airlock and pounds on the door. "Ship!" she yells at the ceiling. "Move us toward the nearest station airlock. Open this hatch! The teachers and crew—they're still out there!"

"I'M SORRY," the ship says. "BUT I CAN'T DO THAT. THIS ENTIRE QUADRANT OF THE STATION HAS BEEN COMPROMISED. OXYGEN

LEVELS ARE BELOW CRITICAL. ALL GRAVI-
TATIONAL RINGS ARE OFFLINE."

Riya gasps. "Are the teachers okay? Did they—"

"I DON'T THINK ANYONE WAS LEFT IN THE
CORRIDOR WHEN IT BLEW," the ship says. "BUT I
DON'T KNOW FOR SURE."

Riya's still punching the door, her fists and cheeks
bright red. "But we can't leave without them!"

Becka walks up to her. "We have to, Riya! We can't
help them now! We're—"

"Alone," Diana finishes. She's standing with Hunter
and Jan Coates, who all look like they've been hit with
a stun blast.

The ship rocks back and forth. I grab the wall to steady
myself, but at least a third of the kids stumble to the floor.

"ANY DAY NOW, FOLKS," the ship says. "THAT
WASN'T A DIRECT HIT, BUT WE NEED TO GET
OUT OF HERE."

Riya and Diana look at Becka. Becka looks at me.
Ari too. And Ming and Cal and Missi and Gena. Everyone. Waiting.

I place my hand on the nearest access panel. "Ship?
Raise shields."

"DONE."

"Missi?" I ask. She turns to me, eyes glassy. "I need
your help."

She's muttering Mr. Cardegna's galaxy map memory
trick over and over. "Three Purple Ninjas Outwitted

Nine Scary Carnivorous Octopi. Three Purple Ninjas Outwitted Nine Scary Carnivorous Octopi. Three Purple Ninjas—"

"Missi!"

She wipes her eyes, bites the insides of her cheeks, and stops chanting. "I'm here."

I smile at her, just as the ship is hit again. "You're in charge of the other eighth graders. Let me know if anyone's missing or hurt."

She nods again. "Got it."

"Great. Ming?"

"What do you need?" they say back. Cool and collected. I'm grateful.

"You're in charge of seventh grade. Same thing."

"Aye, aye, Captain."

I look at Ari and Becka, then back at Ming. "Let's keep it informal."

They nod. "Got it."

"Riya? You've got sixth."

"Okay," Riya responds. "Should we stay in the hangar bay in case we need to escape on the shuttles?"

Missi wipes her eyes. "No, it's safer in the mess hall. Even if we won't be able to evacuate as quickly."

"You're right," I say. "Good instincts." Missi smiles a little. Riya nods without argument. "Take everyone there, strap into the high-velocity chairs, and keep comms open. If any of you need to reach Ari and Becka and me, we'll be on the bridge. Go!"

The ship shivers again. But it's more muted this time. Another blast from outside, hitting against the shields. Becka, Ari, and I bolt upstairs from the hangar bay, through the school, and into the new command bridge. It's bright and gleaming. Every inch of it covered in brand new, top-of-the-line tech. The viewscreen is triple its old size, and the three operations stations have been reconstructed into spherical command pods that read your movements and practically connect your mind to the rest of the ship. But the basic layout is still the same. Three stations: flight, comms/sensors, and the captain's chair.

I don't hesitate. "Ship, give Arizona Bowman and Beckenham Pierce unrestricted access to all systems, including the light speed engine."

"PLAYING NICE THIS TIME AROUND, EH?"

I go even further, typing a set of commands into my station. I'm not making the same mistakes I made last year. We're a team now. A crew. "From here on out, if we want to use the light speed engine, all three of us have to agree on where to go."

The ship chimes, "UNANIMITY LOCK CON-FIRMED," sounding impressed.

I point at the captain's chair. "Go on, Ari. It's yours."

He beams but shakes his head. "No, I couldn't."

"Please just—"

"Okay!" He hops into the center pod without another second's hesitation. The sphere turns 360 degrees as it registers Ari's biochemical imprint. I settle in at flight controls. Becka takes her place at comms and doesn't even complain.

"Well," I say, pulling backward on the new holographic flight lever. "Here goes nothing."

I don't have the best grades in Rudimentary Flight Skills. I can't come close to matching Ari at takeoffs and landings. And no one's better than Becka at close-quarters maneuvering. But I can do this. I know I can.

The ship jerks and we speed away too fast, spinning upward and looping around. We nearly crash back against the station before I level us out.

I can do this. Even if I can't necessarily do it *well*.

A pair of fighters passes overhead, spitting laser fire at the top of our hull. The shields shimmer and vibrate, but nothing gets through.

"*SHIELDS AT EIGHTY-SIX PERCENT,*" the ship notes. "*BUT THEY WON'T HOLD FOREVER.*"

"Can we use the light speed engine now?" I ask.

"*NO. THEY'RE PUMPING OUT THAT SAME JAMMING WE ENCOUNTERED AROUND ELVIDIAN PLANETS. UNTIL WE CAN GET BEYOND ITS RANGE, WE'RE NOT GOING ANYWHERE.*"

"Wonderful," Becka deadpans, swiping at something only she can see from her station. "I'm detecting the outer edge of the jamming. Tossing up a marker."

On the new viewscreen, a hologram materializes

in the distance—Becka's virtual "marker." It's a flashing yellow line with the words "THIS FAR!" hovering above it, next to a few panicked-face emojis. The border between us and escape.

"Becka?!" Ari shouts, spinning around in the captain's chair. "Isn't there something else you can do?!"

A huge grin blooms on her face. "Oh yeah!" she whoops, reaching her hands out in front her, grabbing at the pod's holographic displays. "Ship, full weapons array. Give me bowside Piercer control and EMP laser cannons, port and starboard."

"*NOW WE'RE TALKIN'!*" the ship responds.

Becka's arms whirl inside her station as she makes the command motions to attack the ships around us. One after another, robot fighters spark and explode. Becka is clearing a path between us and the end of the light speed jamming. I maneuver as best I can through the cloud of enemy ships, while Ari monitors ship status, adjusting shield concentrations to compensate for the evil robot fleet.

"Ship," Ari calls, "shield status."

"*AT SIXTY-EIGHT PERCENT. BUT—*"

We're thrown off course, jolted backward and down.

"*SOMETHING'S GOT US,*" the ship tells us. "*MORE OF THOSE MAGLEV TOW CABLES, I THINK.*"

I floor the thrust, hoping to break free. No luck. "They're too strong!" I shout.

"Becka," Ari says, "what about the aft rail gun—er, I mean, the aft *Piercer*?"

She swipes and zooms. "At this angle, it'd cut right through our own thrusters. Even I'm not that good a shot. It's too close-range. Also—incoming transmission." She projects the visual in a corner of the viewscreen.

"Friends!" the robot emperor booms. "Why the betrayal?"

"Betrayal?!" I shout back at the screen. "It's *you* who betrayed *us*!"

Ari looks back at me from the center chair. "Sorry," I mouth. Didn't mean to upstage the captain.

Ari nods and faces forward. "With all due respect, emperor, we don't have time for you to *drone* on and on. Time to *cut through* the nonsense."

He turns and winks at me before spinning back around to face the screen.

"Your tiny minds." The emperor holds up a thumb and forefinger, barely a centimeter apart. "So so tiny. They're no match for our superior networked intelligence. And—"

"Yeah, yeah," Ari interrupts. "I heard Chucklebot Seven's set. But I'm not worried about us. I think you're the one who's at the end of your *rope*." Another wink in my direction.

"Do you have any idea what he's talking about?" Becka whispers.

"I was hoping *you* knew," I say.

Ari overhears us. "Seriously?! Ugh." He glares at the viewscreen, swiping the air to shut down the connection. "PSS 118, out."

As soon as the emperor's face disappears, Ari spins around. "Use the fleet of construction drones parked in Hangar Dock C to cut through the cables! If they can slice clean through graphene paneling, they can for sure cut those ropes."

Becka and I look at each other again.

"Now!" Ari shrieks. "That's an order!"

We don't have to be told twice. Or, we don't have to be told three times, anyway.

"Drones away!" Becka announces.

"I've got 'em," I say, flying the swarm of remote-controlled robots out through one of the smaller hangar ports. "Light the cables up for me, Becka, okay?"

"Gotcha covered," she says.

The black-on-starry-black cables shine bright pink on my screen as Becka highlights them with the ship's sensor package. One by one, I cut through the cables. *Snap*: Still at full thrust, we bank hard to one side. *Snap*: We veer to the other. *Snap. Snap. Snap.* And we're free.

"Jack!" Ari shouts. "Punch it!"

"Aye, aye, Captain," I say, again pulling the holographic throttles as far as they'll go, heading for the edge of that jamming.

"Ten seconds!" Becka counts down.

"Where should we go?" Ari asks.

Principal Lochner's voice echoes in my head. I press a hand down on my access panel, giving the ship permission to unlock the light speed engine. "We finish the mission."

"Five seconds!" Becka tells us, pressing down on her own panel. "We finish the mission."

Ari sits back in the captain's chair. "Agreed all around. Three, two, one. Ship, engage the light speed engine. Destination: The Great Library of the Wyzard System. Now!"

* * *

Moments after leaving the battle, we reappear seventy light years away, near the water-planet of Wyzardia, a shining blue marble that—according to the map we're using—houses the largest library in the galaxy.

I breathe a sigh of relief. Becka hops up to give Ari a hug. I join in. It's hard not to celebrate with my crew. We're one step closer to figuring out the Quarantine and—

"Okay," Hunter says, while we're still in our group hug. "If I wasn't nauseous before, I am now. Either way, I'm gonna need you three to go."

We turn around. Hunter's standing at the back of the command bridge, with his band of merry bullies. Madison and Kingston and Jan, obviously. But the Salinas too. Leigh Lucia and Dan Pavan. Even . . . Diana Pierce. All armed with stun weapons. Pointed right at us.

"What do you think you're doing?" Becka demands, clenching her fists. The question is as much for Diana as it is for Hunter. The younger Pierce sister lowers her eyes.

"What does it look like I'm doing?" Hunter answers, casually waving his blaster around. "I'm taking over the ship."

I steal a moment to glance out the viewscreen.

The library planet is right in front of us.

We're so close.

Did we really escape the battle only to lose the war?

Like this?

I glance at Ari and Becka. She sighs. "Told you it was Hunter."

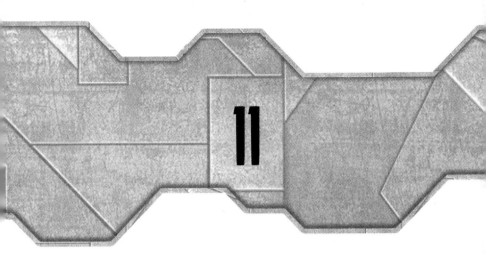

11

"We've really got to stop getting captured," Ari says. "It's embarrassing."

Hard to disagree with him on that one. We're trapped in Classroom 2, in the section of the school that Hunter now calls the brig. Half the student body is being held in one of the classrooms or in the library. Which is something, I guess. Not everyone's willing to go along with our new overlord.

Hunter has stationed two guards outside each classroom. And from the sound of it, I'm guessing that the rest of the pro-Hunter 118ers are somewhere close. The mess hall, maybe? The gym? They seem to be having a party. The 118's walls are usually soundproof, so the music must be pretty loud.

"Hey!" Madison knocks on the classroom window, holding up a plate. "You want pizza?"

Ari darts to the door and interlocks his fingers, begging. "Yes! Please! Pizza! That'd be great."

For a second, Madison smiles. Ari beams at her, and I can actually hear his stomach rumble. But her grin turns cruel and she folds the slice in half, gulping it down in three bites. "Whoops," she says, spitting crust crumbs at the door. "Guess there's no more!"

She disappears from the window, loudly cackling all the way down the corridor. Ari slumps to the floor, his back against the wall. "Guess I should've seen that coming."

Becka shakes her head. "None of us saw any of this coming. Diana . . . betraying us like that? For the *Minister?*"

"I don't know," I say. "I still don't think it was Hunter who sold us out to the Elvidians. He's not smart enough to reprogram the ship's personality matrix to keep it from flying. Also, I mean, listen!" I'm silent for a moment as the bass from some song I almost recognize seeps through the walls. "Would the aliens really spy on us for months, imprison us in a station full of evil robots, and hijack our ship—all so Hunter could party and stuff his face?"

"There's no point trying to understand someone like Hunter," Becka grunts. "I don't care what his deal is. It doesn't change what we have to do: get out of here and retake the ship."

Fair enough. Ari and I nod.

"But how—" Ari starts, right before the door swings open.

"The boss'll see you now," Kingston says, pointing at me with his blaster. Before I can move, he raises the weapon over my head and shoots the wall, bullseye-ing a poster that Mr. Cardegna put up during last year's book fair: *Read, read, Ganymede!*

"I hate that thing," Kingston mutters.

"It hates you back," Becka says, which I think she knows isn't her cleverest burn.

Kingston walks me out into the corridor, relocking the door behind us.

The 118 is a *mess*. And we've only been locked up for a couple of hours. Hunter's accomplices have unfurled rolls of toilet paper and tossed them over the lockers. There are pizza crusts and empty cups and Gushers wrappers everywhere.

Missi Tinker's face stares out at me from Classroom 4. Ming's and Riya's too, from Classroom 5. At least I was right before about who to trust.

Kingston leads me to the gym.

They must have sacked the kitchen. It's practically snowing potato chips. And they've even dragged one of the new food printers in here. It's automatically spitting out slices of pizza like a T-shirt cannon, way more than anyone could eat. And—because they've also turned down the gravity—the slices are clumping together in the air, hot cheese and tomato sauce painting the bleachers. Music is blaring. Kids are dancing and cartwheeling and playing no-rules, you-can-hit-people-in-the-face dodgeball. Diego Pinkerton is DJing in the air, two-thirds of the way up to the ceiling.

Diego's not even a bad kid. We aren't close friends, but we roomed together last spring. He's never been mean. He's never followed Hunter around. But now, here he is, partying with the rest of the mutineers. I notice that he's wearing an old PSS uniform polo shirt—except he's ripped off the sleeves, which I can't help but think is the thing Principal Lochner would like the least about this whole day.

Principal Lochner. Who led us down one wrong path after another.

I'm not saying that this is all his fault. But we wouldn't be in this situation—without the teachers, controlled by a kid who thinks that tripping people in the hallway is the funniest joke in the universe—if our principal had been more careful.

I don't care for Hunter's methods. Obviously. But he was right about one thing: the teachers dropped the ball. And now *Hunter LaFleur* is in charge of the last free human spaceship in the galaxy.

"This way," Kingston says, leaping through the low-gravity air of the gym.

Jan Coates floats down to me. "Aw, did little baby Jackie wanna captain the ship again? Wah wah!" She traces fake tears on her cheeks with her fingers. "Too bad!"

Jan kicks off the floor to propel herself back upward.

Halfway to the ceiling, she plucks a carton of orange juice from the air, drinks half of it, and leaves the rest of it floating there, uncapped. A stream of perfectly good juice floats up and out of the carton.

"How's Becka?"

I turn. It's Diana, magboots on her feet to keep her grounded.

"She's fine," I say. "No thanks to you."

Diana frowns. "I know Hunter can be a jerk. But look around! We're safe. We're having fun. We just escaped literally the scariest thing I've ever experienced. And now you and Becka and Ari want to plunge into some hopeless mission on a planet we know nothing about? We're only kids!"

I open my mouth, hoping to come up with a decent response. But I draw a blank.

"Keep it moving, Jack," Kingston says.

He flies to the other side of the room, and I follow, feeling Diana's gaze on me until we're through the doors and in the quieter, full-gravity portside hallway.

Kingston leads me around the corner and into Principal Lochner's office. What used to be Principal Lochner's office, anyway. Now it's Hunter's, um, lair?

"Leave us," Hunter says to Kingston, who quickly shuffles out of the office.

Hunter is sitting—feet up, shoes off—at the principal's desk. He's defaced the *Settle it with a smile!* poster on the back wall by crossing out "smile" and writing in "fart" with a Sharpie. Because Hunter's nothing if not consistent.

He's got six cartons of melting ice cream open in front of him, BUT ONLY ONE SPOON. That monster. The vanilla's all chocolatey. The strawberry's green with pistachio. And . . . are those raisins in the regular chocolate?!

Hunter's poisoned the chocolate ice cream with *raisins.*

He must be stopped.

"Welcome!" he tells me, stretching his arms and burping. "Welcome to Hunter's new digs." Naturally, he now refers to himself in third person. "I'm so glad you could make it."

"You didn't exactly give me a choice," I point out, collapsing into one of the two chairs opposite him.

I hear more voices behind me, low and muffled. I turn. A dozen screens have been mounted on the front wall of the office. One shows the party in the gym. Another displays some kids exploding paint cans in the mess hall. And of course, there are monitors for everyone locked up in the classrooms. I see Missi, running her hands along the air vent in Classroom 4 for some reason. Riya is screaming at a startled Diego Pinkerton through the door of Classroom 5, while Ming stands in the back of the room, running their own hands along the walls. I zero in on Classroom 2: Becka and Ari, talking about something. Ari's crying. And I think I make out the word "celery," which probably means he's worried about

Doctor Shrew. Becka awkwardly pats him on the back in a *there, there* motion.

"Gotta keep an eye on my ship," Hunter says with a shrug. He licks his one spoon, stabs it into the carton of vanilla, and slides it across the desk. "Ice cream?"

"No thanks."

He wipes his sticky mouth on the *GO PSS 118 CHAMPIONS!* sweatshirt draped over the back of Principal Lochner's chair and tosses the sweatshirt on the floor. "So Jack," he says. "Can I call you Jack?"

"You're terrible," I tell him.

He nods. "Everyone's terrible. Some people just aren't afraid to admit it. Anyway, I'll get to the point. We're on our own now. And, like I've already said, there's no way I'm gonna waste my freedom on a library." He chuckles, like the idea couldn't be more ridiculous. "A library!"

"And?" I ask.

Hunter crosses his arms. "Come on," he says. "You know we've lost. All the other humans are gone. And now Lochner and the teachers and crew are gone too."

"You don't know that," I say. But I can hear the doubt in my own voice.

"Hmmm. Let's see. Last we saw them, they were getting overrun by an army of robots. Best case scenario: They're trapped in our solar system with no light speed engine. How long do you think our old lunch robots can keep them safe, huh? You think that because Stingy once made an okay meatloaf, the robot can win a war?"

"Stingy's meatloaf was less than okay," is all I say back. "And its battle strategy is even worse."

"So what do you want with *me*?" I ask.

Hunter grins, stands up, and presses a hand against one of the ship's interface panels behind the desk.

"*JACK IS RIGHT*," the ship says. "*YOU ARE TERRIBLE*."

"I've managed to take control of most systems," Hunter tells me over his shoulder. I can hear the grimace in his voice. "Including basic ship AI commands, even if we can't seem to shake off the ship's annoying personality. Unfortunately."

"*I AM RUBBER, YOU ARE GLUE*," the ship says.

Hunter turns back to me and rolls his eyes. "Nice. Classy. Anyway, Diana Pierce is pretty good with computers." Maybe she is, maybe she isn't. I get the feeling that Hunter is saying her name to gloat. "But the one important thing we can't seem to operate is your little light speed engine."

So *that's* why I'm here. Only Ari, Becka, and I can get us out of this system. To wherever it is Hunter thinks we should go instead.

"Ship," Hunter says, "show us Planet 10191."

"*SURE THING, HUNTY*."

Hunter winces. He does *not* like that nickname. Which I may need to remember for later.

The ship displays a hologram of a tiny planet—or maybe a moon—in the foreground of a purple-pink gas giant. The planet is clearly populated, sparkling with city lights on its surface.

"According to the Elvidian map, this is the funnest place in the galaxy. Transdimensional roller coasters. Hologames where time literally stops, so you can play forever without getting old or needing to eat or whatever. And the food! It's—"

I'm not listening. Because on the now-active ship access panel, words are coming together. The light is low, probably so Hunter won't notice and turn back around.

JACK! IT'S THE SHIP! GET TO THE BRIDGE. GET INSIDE THE COMMAND PODS. THEN

"Are you even hearing me?!" Hunter says, snapping his fingers in front of my face. "Moon to Jack. Moon to Jack. Come in, Jack!"

Hunter maybe catches something suspicious in my expression. He whips around, but the ship erases the words on the screen before he can see them. Hunter touches the panel anyway. "Buh-bye for now, Ship. Go away." He turns back to me and adds: "I hate the ship. Don't you? I wish I didn't need the AI at all. But what can you do?"

Hunter reaches under the desk and pulls out a rectangular case. "As a gesture of goodwill," he says, setting the case next to the ice cream cartons, "I'm giving you back Bowman's stupid hamster. Call it an olive branch. We can all get what we want and not waste the time we have left on doomed missions planned by teachers who got outsmarted by Captain Hookbot."

"Thanks," I mumble, still staring at the now-blank access panel. The ship wants Hunter out of the captain's chair as much as I do. As much as I did. But—and I can't believe I'm even thinking this—should we just let Hunter get his way? Is the Great Library even worth it? We could stay on the ship. Or maybe visit the fun planet. Stay safe. Keep out of trouble.

Or we could do down to the surface of Wyzardia and risk everything because our middle school principal thought it was a good idea.

"So?" Hunter asks, picking a raisin out from between his teeth. "You gonna help me or what?"

ARI'S LOG: DAY 175
(OR DAY 2 OF THE REIGN OF KING
LAFLEUR THE TERRIBLE)

Hunter gave me back my journal. And freed Doctor Shrew! So for the record: If he thinks he can buy my loyalty this way . . . well, it's not the worst idea he's ever come up with, to be honest. Doctor Shrew's just <u>too cute</u>. Look at that face! But I know it's a trick. Hunter doesn't do anything for anyone unless he wants something in return. And in this case, we know exactly what that is. Jack told us the second he came back from their meeting. Hunter wants to scrap the mission and take the ship to a space carnival or something? And hey, no one's more up for a space carnival than yours truly. I'll take a victory lap on an alien carousel any day of the week. But not until <u>after</u> we save humanity.

   After Jack brought us up to speed, I asked him what the plan was. But he just glanced at the ceiling and said, "I need to think." Which was when Becka said, "You're not actually considering helping him, are you?" And Jack said, "I don't know!" And Becka said, "I can't believe you!" And Jack said, "I haven't decided yet!" And Becka got in Jack's face and was all like, "Well, it doesn't matter. Because you turned on the unanimity lock. So he needs all three of us to engage the engine." Jack shook his head and looked at the ceiling again for some reason and said, "Can we please stop talking about this for a little while?" Becka threw up her hands and said, "I'll talk all I want!" So I got between them and was like, "Hey, can we please stop fighting? Maybe they'll at least bring us pizza if we're good."

ARI'S LOG: DAY 176 (OR, DAY 3 OF THE REIGN OF KING LAFLEUR THE STILL-NOT-GREAT, PROBABLY)

Okay. Hear me out. I'm not on his side now or anything. But they really did bring us pizza! Kingston delivered a whole pie last night, after the blackout. (The lights went dark for twenty minutes for some reason. Maybe just in our room, who knows.) When I asked if they had any olive slices, he came back like a minute later with a _second_ pie, all olive. (Black olives. But good effort.) I ate at least five slices all by myself. Of course, Becka pointed out, "They're trying to bribe us. You get that, right?" And I got it, one hundred percent. Didn't mean I couldn't enjoy the bribe, though.

I started in on my journal after dinner, and Jack said, "You can probably stop doing that now. It matters even less than before." "Not to me," I said—at literally the exact same second Becka, from her corner, said, "Not to him."—and we stared at each other for two seconds before I had to look away. Now I think I'm going to stop writing and go to bed anyway. Because I've suddenly got a heavy feeling in my chest from, you know, all the pizza. Yeah, that's it. It's the pizza. For sure.

ARI'S LOG: DAY 177 (OR, DAY 4 OF THE REIGN OF KING LAFLEUR THE KIND-OF-OKAY?)

Look, Hunter is Hunter is Hunter. I know. I also know that he could be treating us worse. This is definitely the best imprisonment we've had. Hungry for more pizza? Here's three more pies! Ice cream for breakfast? Have all the flavors! Miss playing video games? Hunter rigged Classroom 3 into a remote Neptune Attacks sim and lets us play whenever we want, volume as high as it goes. (During one run for the Sixth Singularity Obelisk, it was so loud that I even thought I heard blaster fire in the hallway. But that was probably just Becka's new dinosaur cyborg avatar, T-Bex Machina.) Of course, I'm still not gonna go along with Hunter's plan.

I mean, unless Becka and Jack go along with it. And that's never gonna happen, right?

ARI'S LOG: DAY 178
(OR, DAY 5 OF THE REIGN OF KING LAFLEUR THE—WELL, YOU'LL SEE)

Channeling his best robot emperor, Hunter invited us to a party in the gym. "Come on in! Welcome to the first annual PSS 118—" He turned to Madison. "Did we change that yet?"

Madison shook her head. "Someone renamed it 'The Ganymede' last year. Diana hasn't been able to figure out how to adjust the transponder a second time." Becka grinned.

"Whatever," Hunter said. "Anyway, as I was saying, welcome to the first annual ship holiday banquet!"

I took it all in. The gym had been cleaned and decorated, although you could still see some tomato sauce stains on the linoleum floor. Someone had hung tinsel and twinkling white lights from the rafters in the ceiling. I spotted a fake Christmas tree in the corner, cluttered with small ornaments of—I had to blink twice to believe it—Hunter's head. The bleachers had also been lowered into the floor, replaced by a mountain of 3D-printed fake snow. And several long tables were set up on the half-court line.

"Why are we here, Hunter?" Becka asked.

Hunter smiled. "It's the holidays! We should celebrate together."

Becka rolled her eyes. "We're not falling for it. You can butter us up all you want."

Jack opened his mouth to say something but stayed quiet. And I didn't want to leave Becka without backup, so I added, "Besides, I'm Jewish. I don't even celebrate Christmas!"

Hunter smiled even wider. "I know! We've represented a wide range of winter holiday traditions. Including Hanukkah." He pointed at one of the tables.

That's when I saw the menorah—candles lit with electronic bulbs—surrounded by trays of jelly doughnuts, latkes, and chocolate coins (with Hunter's face on the gold and silver wrapping).

Hunter put a hand on my shoulder and said, "May Sol burn brightly till the end. Is that a traditional Hanukkah greeting? Because it totally should be."

"You're so right!" I practically squealed, probably louder than I should have.

Becka put her hand on my other shoulder. "He's not falling for your tricks, Hunter."

"Oh, yeah," I said, filling up a plate anyway. "For sure. You can't buy me with a pile of jelly doughnuts."

"Actually," Hunter explained, "they're half caramel." Which are my _favorite_. But I was worried that Becka would slap them out of my hands if I said that out

113

loud, so I tried to play it cool and loaded up on <u>both</u> kinds of doughnuts to be safe.

Becka rolled her eyes at me and said, "He's trying to manipulate you! Don't you get it? Doctor Shrew. The food. The video games. This whole party. It's all for you, because Hunter thinks you're . . . you know . . . the weak one."

I took a step back. Suddenly I wasn't hungry. (Actually, that's not true. But I did stop chewing for a few seconds.) "And what's that supposed to mean?!"

"I'm sorry," she said, like she had to. "It's just—"

I sat down at the banquet table. "Forget it. I probably wouldn't understand. Because I'm so weak."

There were place cards by every seat. Mine put me between Hunter—at the very head of the table— and Jan Coates on my left. Becka and Jack were all the way down at the other end. In between us were Madison and Kingston, the Salinas, and Dan Pavan. And once everyone was seated, Hunter leaned in close to me and whispered, "Hey, buddy. I don't mean to pry. But does she always talk to you like that?"

ARI'S LOG: DAY 178 (PART II)

Sorry, got interrupted. Lots going on. Where's a time machine when you need one?

Back to the party: "Thank you all for coming," Hunter said after a sixth-grader, Albi Butler, passed

114

around appetizers of Dunkaroos, fries, and cheese curls. "I know that some of you still don't see things my way. But I'm hoping that I can try again to explain what I want to do and why I think it's the right thing. All I'm asking is that you hear me out and—"

The lights went out.

What happened next is a jumble. It was pitch black—not even starlight, since there are no windows in the gym. Someone screamed. I heard a familiar rumble: The bleachers mechanically rose up and out of the floor. Glass spilled off the table and shattered on the ground. Kingston shouted something like, "Get off me!" And then the lights turned back on: Hunter, Kingston, Madison, and Jan were gathered in a line, backs against one of the walls. Guarded by Ming, Riya, Missi, Cal, and Gena, who were pointing stun blasters right at them. I glanced at Jack and Becka. Their eyes were lit up brighter than the menorah. Behind me, Dan Pavan—a double agent!—had his own blaster trained on the Salinas.

"It's over," Riya said. "No more games."

Ming—who'd obviously been through some stuff; you could see it in their eyes—got in Kingston's face. "Hope you enjoy the brig as much as we did," they said.

Gena started herding Madison toward the door.

And Hunter . . . clapped. A slow, sarcastic, not-a-good-sign clap. "Impressive," he said, turning his head to Jack and Becka. "Did you know about

115

them? They've been giving me trouble for days. Cutting power. Sneaking around the air vent system. Starting skirmishes in the corridors. They even spray-painted pictures of the stupid hamster all over the ship."

"Wait," I interrupted, looking at Ming. "Is Doctor Shrew a symbol of resistance?! Please tell me Doctor Shrew is a symbol of resistance."

(Note to self: Install high-beam Shrew signal on the front of the 118.)

"I didn't know that Dan was the mole," Hunter continued, gearing up for another bad-guy speech. "And I admit to having trouble flushing out Ming, Riya, and the rest." Hunter whistled, and the doors on both sides of the gym burst open. "Lucky for me, no one can resist a good party."

It was over in seconds. More kids marched in, laser rifles in hand. Ming reached for their own blaster. But they were hit immediately, stunned out cold. Dan, Gena, and Cal went down too. Madison tackled Riya to the ground. And Missi just tossed her blaster to the side, raising her hands in surrender.

"You knew we were coming?" Riya asked, once Hunter's soldiers rounded up the rebels.

"We were the bait," Becka said, her face falling.

Hunter smiled and nodded at Kingston. "Get them out of here, except for Bowman, Graham, and Pierce." Then he walked closer to us, still out of breath from the battle. "So come on," Hunter said, wiping the sweat off his forehead with his palm and extending the same gross hand for Jack to shake. "Help me use the light speed engine to get us out of here. There's no other choice. You can see that, right? I've got this whole ship on lock."

And Jack—who'd been first to insist we finish the mission after we escaped the robots, who'd led us out of the Elvid System last summer when all hope seemed lost, who was the last person I'd have guessed would give up—gave up.

"Yeah," he said, shaking Hunter's hand. "I'll help."

"What?!" I blurted out. "You will?!"

Becka took a big step forward, so I took a bigger step back. I knew she was gonna give both of them a piece of her mind and I didn't want to be within fist-swinging distance.

But she was disappointing me in all kinds of ways today. "Yeah," she said, gaze to the floor. "Me too."

"Hey!" I shouted, waving my arms in her face, not caring that Hunter could hear me. "This is Hunter LaFleur we're talking about. You can't be serious. We're not really doing this, are we?"

Becka locked eyes with me. "Yeah," she said. "We're really doing this. It's over."

13

Of course we weren't really doing this. Who do you think I am? (Also, don't tell Ari I sneaked a peak at his journal when he wasn't looking, 'kay? I just wanted to make sure he wasn't too mad at me. But I can handle "disappointed." I'll come back from "disappointed." You'll see.)

Also, this is Becka's log. In case you still don't recognize the sound of my voice.

"Hunter's right," Jack said. I couldn't believe he was giving in like that. "We don't have any other choice."

"I agree," I lied. "Let's get this over with."

Poor Ari's jaw dropped all the way down to the gym floor. If only there'd been some way to let him know it was all an act. But Hunter was watching closely. And I had to convince him that I'd finally switched sides. I looked over at Jack and nodded. He nodded back. The traitor.

Ari shook his head and threw up his hands. "Okay, I guess. If you two are in, I am too. But I'm noting in my journal that you both gave up first. For the record."

Hunter clasped his stupid hands together. "Fantastic. No time like the present, right?"

Jack gritted his teeth. At least he wasn't enjoying being a sellout. "May as well."

We stepped into the corridor, Hunter leading the way. Have I ever told you about how Hunter walks? Uch. Head up. Shoulders back. Arms out. Chin as high as it goes. Guy struts around like he owns the place. And every other place too. It's so annoying.

"We're on your side now," I told him. "I've seen the light or whatever. So you can call off your goons."

Madison and Kingston were still in the hallway, armed. It looked like they were gonna accompany us to the command bridge too. Jack and Ari and I probably could've taken Hunter alone, right then and there. But I didn't like the three-on-three odds. Four-on-two, I guess, now that Jack had fallen in line.

"Better safe than sorry," Hunter said. "You three get us to the fun planet, I'll give you run of the ship. No problem. For now, you've got to prove your loyalty."

As we walked toward the bridge, we passed a few kids lying in the hallway, faces covered in cake, groaning and clutching their stomachs. Albi Butler—who'd bolted from the gym when the lights cut out—was standing in a corner, pouring seltzer onto his cheese-curl-stained shirt, rubbing it with shredded napkins.

"Hey, Hunter!" Albi called out. "Can we use the washing machines?"

"What?" Hunter said, knocking Albi to the side with his shoulder. "Sure, use literally whatever you want. I don't care."

Albi called after him: "But where *are* the washing machines?"

"Not now, Albi."

"But—"

Hunter lifted his blaster and *shot Albi in the chest*. He fell to the ground in a pool of cheesy seltzer, and even Madison and Kingston stopped to stare at their fearless leader. Because there it was, plain as day: Hunter could give all the fancy speeches he wanted. He could talk about trying to do what he thought was right. Blah blah blah. But the truth is, Hunter's just a scared kid, only looking out for himself, not caring how many annoying sixth graders he has to blast out of his way.

"Don't look at me like that," Hunter snapped. "He'll be fine. It's on like the lowest stun setting. Now move it."

When we reached the command bridge, our odds got worse. There were even more of Hunter's cronies in here. Diego Pinkerton was slumped in the captain's chair, spinning in circles, looking bored. Jan Coates was writing her name on the walls in permanent marker, practicing her cursive: *Jankari Coates. Jankari Coates. Jankari Coates.* And Diana . . .

Diana.

She was hunched over one of the ship's access panels, fiddling with some wires she'd yanked out from an open socket. I marched over to her.

Diana.

That—

"Backstabbing, lying, spineless . . . Newton's cannon-ball!" Trust me, if you took Mr. Cardegna's seventh grade astrophysics final, you'd know what a sick burn that was.

Tears pooled in her eyes.

"Yeah, you'd *better* cry," I said, which I regret. A little. Heat of the moment.

I almost grabbed her into a headlock to prove my point. But Hunter got between us first. "Ladies, ladies, please," he said. And I suddenly remembered with the fire of a thousand burning Wolf-Rayet stars who *really* deserved a headlock. But it wasn't time. Not yet.

"Sorry," I muttered. "We're all on the same side now."

That seemed to startle Diana a little. "We are?"

At least *she* knew *me* well enough to know where I'd stand. Wish that made two of us.

"We sure are," Hunter said, rubbing his palms together. "So get to it."

I scanned the bridge for possibilities. We were outnumbered pretty badly, so a direct confrontation was out of the question. I still wanted to tackle Diana, but that probably wouldn't have gotten us any closer to retaking the ship.

The ship.

If I could get close to an access panel, maybe I could at least throw Hunter's operation into a little chaos. Unlock all the doors. Free the Shrew Five. Even the odds a little.

Problem was, I was out of time.

"Becka, Ari, and I just need to take our stations," Jack was explaining. "Then we can use the light speed engine."

"Wait. What?" Ari asked. "Why do we need the command pods? Can't we just use voice controls to deactivate the unanimity lock?"

Hunter squinted at Ari, then at Jack. "If this is a trick, Graham, I'll drop you off on the nearest moon. Oxygen or no oxygen."

"I know," Jack said, glaring at Ari. "No tricks."

Hunter looked at Ari for confirmation. Ari just shrugged. "No one's got a better sense of the ship than Jack. Becka and I wouldn't have any access if not for him. If he says we need to be in the stations, we need to be in the stations."

Jack breathed a sigh of relief. Good old Ari. Making even traitors feel better about themselves.

But he was right about one thing: No one knows the ship better than Jack. Which meant that I had a new target.

Diego got up and offered Jack the captain's pod. Ari stepped toward flight. And I made my move.

Slam.

Tackled Jack to the ground.

Wham.

Locked his arms behind his back.

Bam.

Back up, holding Jack's body as a shield between me and Hunter's raised blaster.

"What are you doing?!" Jack shrieked.

"What does it look like I'm doing? I'm not letting you take this ship anywhere. We have a mission on that planet." I tilted my head toward the viewscreen. "And we're going to complete it."

Hunter laughed. "Why am I not surprised?" He turned to Diana. "Told you she couldn't be trusted."

Diana winced. Meanwhile Jack wriggled to the side and mumbled into my ear. Something like, "I'm on a slide!" But the words were hard to make out. I was squeezing him pretty tight.

"What's your plan, Becka?" Hunter asked. "You've got no weapons. You're alone up here."

I shook my head. Just had to keep him talking a little longer. "Wrong. My weapon is right here." I pointed at Jack's head with my one free hand. "You shoot me, you shoot Jack. We're not going anywhere without Jack. And as for being alone, well, sisters before misters, if you know what I mean."

Hunter groaned. "Guess I shouldn't have trusted you either," he said, realizing that Diana had sneaked up behind him, her own stun weapon aimed at his back.

"Becka, I'm sorry!" Diana called out, craning her neck to see around Hunter.

I nodded, tearing up a little. But like, a perfectly reasonable amount of tears for the moment. Five to ten, tops. "I know."

"I just wanted to do something big. Something important. Like you."

"I love you!" I shouted across the bridge, elbow around Jack's windpipe.

Diana beamed. "Love you too, Bex," she answered, blaster pressed into Hunter's back.

Classic sister stuff.

Hunter gagged. "Blech. Leave *me* on the nearest moon if you're gonna be so gross. Besides, I don't see how this changes anything. Diana stuns me. Kingston and Madison stun you and Jack and Ari—"

"Why do you have to stun *me*?!" Ari yelped.

"Then we start this all over again in an hour. I still have control of the ship and you have, what, the love of your little sister? Whether it's now or tomorrow or a week from now, you'll come around."

"Never," I told him. "There's only one right thing to do here. And it's to finish. The. Mission."

I was getting kind of worked up and accidentally loosened my death grip on Jack. Enough for him to get out what he'd been trying to tell me: "I'm on your side," he gasped. "We need to get into the command pods. All three of us."

So I lost focus for a second. Got distracted. Madison tackled me to floor. And Hunter did a pretty impressive around-the-back blaster-grab from Diana.

"Nice try," Hunter grunted, out of breath, blowing his bangs out of his eyes. "But I'm done with this. Jack, what do you need to get us out of here?"

Madison pulled me up off the floor, and Jack turned

around to look at me. And I'll tell you: I still wasn't sure if I could trust him. He'd sold out, hadn't he? He'd given up, right? I mean, he'd been whining about Principal Lochner and the teachers since before we left Earth. He was buying Hunter's nonsense. And now—he was definitely lying to someone. But was it Hunter, or me?

I made a call. If you can't believe in your friends, you're doomed anyway.

"Okay," I said, drooping my shoulders as far down as they'd go. "I give up. Let's get out of here."

Hunter stepped closer. "Finally! Do your thing, Graham."

"Um," Jack stuttered. "First, I need to ask the ship a question." He placed his hand against the nearest panel. "Ship?"

The panel lit up. "*WHAT DO YOU WANT, TRAITOR?*"

Jack: "Ship, I want to make sure I'm doing this right. Becka and Ari and I need to get *inside* the command pods—and then what? Is there a special code or something?"

"*OH, WOULDN'T YOU LIKE TO KNOW,*" the ship growled. "*YOU'LL NEVER GET AWAY WITH THIS!*"

"We already have, Ship," Hunter said. "Now tell Jackie boy what he needs to know. Or our first stop will be a junkyard. Wonder what we can get for an old pile of bolts with a fresh coat of paint."

"*FINE!*" the ship snapped. "*YES. THE THREE OF THEM JUST NEED TO GET INSIDE THE COMMAND PODS,*

THEN ENGAGE THE ENCLOSURES. MAXIMUM SEAL. THAT SHOULD RESET THE LIGHT SPEED ENGINE IMMEDIATELY. NO SPECIAL CODE REQUIRED."

Seal the enclosures?

No way.

My mind raced: Could they be escape pods?!

"Excellent," Hunter said. "You heard the ship. In you go."

My mind kept racing: *What'll we do when we get to the surface by ourselves? Will Hunter come after us? Will Diana be okay? Is this a good idea? Are we making a mistake?*

In case you didn't know, my mind actually races like that a lot. It's hard not to worry all the time, even when the fate of the human race *isn't* at stake. I know, I know— Becka Pierce, a worrier?! Just don't tell anyone. I got a rep to maintain.

"Ship?" Jack asked, once we were inside the three pods. "Lower the enclosures, please."

"*FINE,*" the ship said. "*BUT I DON'T HAVE TO LIKE IT.*"

A glass bubble rose up from the bottom of each station and met the half-moon enclosures at the top. Mine sealed around me and I felt my ears pop. I glanced ahead at Jack: His fingers tightly gripping the arm rests. His hands shaking. The back of his neck all sweaty. Jack doesn't do small spaces super well. And Ari? I glanced to the side. Guy was absolutely delighted. Huge smile. Sparkling eyes. He saw me looking at him and gave me a thumbs up, which maybe shouldn't have made me feel any better, but kind of did?

"Is that it?" Hunter asked.

"*LIGHT SPEED ENGINE RESET IN PROCESS*," the ship said. "*YOU JUST HAVE TO PRESS THE IGNITION ON THE ACCESS PANEL TO YOUR LEFT.*" Hunter glanced over at the panel. An image of a big red button appeared on its screen. It said, "For Hunter: Push Here." The 118 was making this incredibly easy for him.

"Well, Becka," Hunter said smugly, pressing his thumb down on the screen. "Looks like you lost again."

Then the bridge lit up with a million electrical sparks that showered down from the ceiling as the ship called out— "*PRIME COUNTERMEASURE LAMDA ACTIVATED.*"— and Hunter and Madison and Kingston and Diego and Diana collapsed onto the floor.

"Diana!" I screamed, pounding my fists on the glass of my command pod.

"*RELAX!*" the ship said as it lowered the pod enclosures. "*THEY'RE FINE! JUST ASLEEP.*"

I ran over to Diana anyway, feeling for a pulse. She snored.

"*REALLY,*" the ship said. "*IT'S OUR MILDEST BOARDING COUNTERMEASURE.*"

"I thought they were escape pods," I mumbled.

Jack nodded. "Me too."

Ari raked his fingers through his hair. "Can someone *please* tell me what side we're on?! This is all very hard to follow!"

Jack and I looked at each other.

"You were never with Hunter?" I asked him.

Jack shook his head. "Nope. You?"

"Nah. Not for a second."

"Me neither," Jack insisted. And I believed him. "When I was called to his office that first day, the ship told me we could use the command pods, somehow. But I couldn't figure out how to tell you. Not with the cameras everywhere."

I slapped my forehead. "I forgot about the cameras! Of course you had to lie!"

"You were lying to me?" Ari asked, looking back and forth between us. "You were *both* lying to me?"

"Technically," I said, "we were also lying to each other."

"Sorry," Jack said. "I did try giving you . . . looks."

Ari's face softened. "Looks?"

Jack widened his eyes maybe twenty percent. "Like this, see? Doesn't my face say: 'Hey, I'm just pretending to go along with Hunter so he'll take us to the bridge and we can retake the ship'?"

Ari gasped. "Oh, so that's what that face means! I thought you had to go to the bathroom!"

Jack leaned in closer to a sleeping Diego Pinkerton. Poked him in the arm. "Principal Lochner never said anything about boarding countermeasures."

"I think Ms. Needle was gonna cover that in the spring semester," Ari said. Then: "Hey, Ship, how long will they be out?"

"*NOT LONG. YOU SHOULD PROBABLY SECURE HUNTER AND THE REST BEFORE THEY WAKE UP.*"

"The brig?" Jack asked me.

I nodded. "The brig."

But Ari still had more questions. "What I don't get," he said, staring at the nearest control panel, "is why Hunter had to press that button. Couldn't one of us have done it from our stations? Or, Ship, couldn't you just have done it yourself?"

"*OH FOR SURE*," the ship answered. "*BUT THAT WOULDN'T HAVE BEEN NEARLY AS MUCH FUN.*"

We all looked at each other, then down at Hunter, who was curled up in a ball on the command bridge floor, sucking his thumb, muttering, "No, Becka, no . . . You're not better than me . . ."

I patted him on the head. "Yeah, I am, buddy."

Best. Day. Ever.

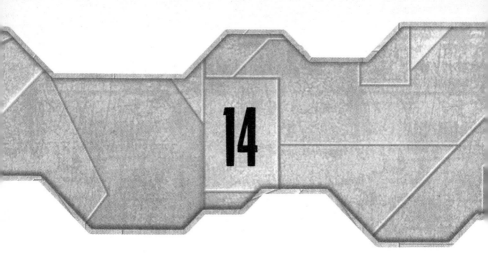

14

Becka kicks a little sand with her foot. "So, this place is great and all . . ."

She's right: blue skies, even bluer ocean, purple palm tree-ish plants swaying in a perfect breeze. The shining sun isn't too hot, and the few wispy green-blue clouds overhead make me feel like I'm in a painting.

"But it doesn't look like a library."

She's right about that too.

We made it. Wyzardia. The planet is almost all ocean, except for a ring of ten thousand islands tracing the equator in a too-perfect circle. Each island is small. Really small. A few city blocks, at most. Doesn't seem like enough real estate for the galaxy's Great Library.

It wasn't hard to get down here. As soon as we fell into orbit with the other ships milling around Wyzardia, we got an audio transmission from the surface. "Welcome," the voice said, the ship's new translation tech working perfectly. "You have been assigned Island

No. 2371 for your library needs. Coordinates attached to this message. Small craft only, please. Thank you."

Finally, on with the mission.

And for the record, I never betrayed Becka and Ari, okay? Yeah, I had my doubts about our mission. Yeah, I was afraid. But if I've learned anything over the last few months, it's this: Even when you're afraid, you can make the right choice.

Also this: Keep Hunter LaFleur where you can see him. Hence the full brig. We didn't lock up *everyone* who went along with the coup. I mean, hasn't poor Albi Butler been through enough? But we did hold an assembly where Becka yelled a lot and Ari made a show of granting amnesty to everyone but the ringleaders. Riya Windsor also set up shop in Dr. Hazelwood's office and has been interrogating all the kids, one by one. She's trying to suss out if anyone still onboard the ship is spying for the Minister. So far, no luck.

We've done some other stuff too. Responsible stuff. Set up a rotating system for the captain's chair, involving rock-paper-scissors and comm ring timers. (My turn now. Becka's up next.) Assigned other roles to the people we trust the most: Missi Tinker's now our official science officer, on account of her being valedictorian last year. Riya is chief of security. Cal Brown and Gena Korematsu are sharing responsibility for looking after the rest of the kids, keeping them busy, continuing their training (a job I am very glad not to have). And Ming's acting captain when Ari, Becka, and I are off the ship. Ming didn't want that job at first. But everybody likes Ming, which makes them the perfect choice to keep the peace. Especially after Hunter's Rebellion.

And finally, here we are. An expedition to the surface of Wyzardia. Me, Ari, Becka, Missi, and Riya.

It's not going great.

"Um, hey, planet?" Missi tries, cupping her hands and shouting into the sky. "Where's the library?"

No answer.

"Worth a try," Ari says, nodding.

"What if I shoot the ground?" Riya offers, charging her blaster rifle.

Becka gives her a thumbs up as I say, "Let's make that a last resort."

Riya keeps the weapon trained on the sand, just in case.

We've already walked the circumference of this island three times. Crisscrossed it twice. But it's only sand, trees, and little crab bugs that scuttle around in packs, dig for shells in the dirt, and yell, "Meep meep!" when you get too close.

No library.

"You know I'm your friend, right?" I say to Ari, as we march along the shore.

"Oh yeah," he answers, munching on a bag of corn chips he brought in his backpack. "Best friend." He swings his backpack around to his chest and glances down apologetically. "Best *human* friend, I mean," he says to Doctor Shrew, who he also brought along. Ari covers Doctor Shrew's ears with his hands. "Sorry," he whispers, glancing up at me. "He's had a hard week."

"I understand. Point is, I'm looking out for you. Which is why I have to say . . . you look ridiculous."

Ari stops in his tracks and looks down at himself. He's wearing a hooded black cloak. *To the beach.* He's even outfitted his Pencil with this long, screw-on extension he's using as a walking stick. I'm pretty sure it's supposed to double as a magic wand.

"*I* look ridiculous?" Ari says, offended. "What about you?"

I'm wearing flip-flops, a flower-patterned bathing suit, and a T-shirt that says, "It's Always Summer on Venus." Perfectly reasonable. But Ari's not gonna budge, so I just push my sunglasses up the bridge of my nose and let it go.

Riya plops down onto the ground. "There's no library here."

Missi and Becka join her. Me and Ari too.

"Maybe it's invisible?" Ari offers, drawing circles in the sand with his scraggly staff.

Missi rolls her eyes, wiggling her fingers like she's telling us a spooky story. "Do you mean, maybe it's magic?"

"I mean, maybe it's *cloaked*," Ari says. "I'm not stupid."

Becka chuckles. "I could've sworn I heard you muttering 'abracadabra' when we first landed."

Ari shrugs. "Might as well cover all the bases."

"Why don't we just ask one of those other ships in orbit?" Missi suggests. "Maybe they know something."

"I don't want to draw any more attention to ourselves than we absolutely have to," I say. "I know this isn't the Elvid System. But still, who knows what the Minister has told people about us? What if, when they realize who we are, they call in the Elvidians?"

Missi nods. "Makes sense, I guess."

"It's just," Ari says, shaking sand out of his hood, "we're here! We got this far. We're the only humans to escape the Quarantine. We've *got* to be able to figure this out."

I open my mouth to respond. But the earthquake hits first.

It starts as a low rumble, deep underground, but it builds quickly. Water rushes up the shore. Waves suddenly crash against the spot where we're sitting, which had been thirty feet from the ocean just seconds ago. We stand up. The ground shakes again. Ari and Missi trip into each other and fall back down. Becka yanks them up to their feet.

"Let's go!" Riya shouts, making a break for the shuttle, halfway across the island. We can see it from here, slowly sinking into the ocean.

Becka grabs Riya by the wrist and points to higher ground. "No! Look!"

There, in the very center of the island, something

is coming up out of the ground. A box of steel and cement.

"This way!" I call to the others, turning toward the box.

"But the shuttle!" Missi shouts.

"Leave it!" I order. "Ming can send another shuttle. We're seeing this through."

Missi hesitates, but only for a moment. "Aye, aye, Captain," she says.

The rumbling slows, but the water is still rising. The whole island is sinking. The shuttle disappears beneath the waves. And we run.

"Move it!" I urge, waving the group forward toward the mysterious box. As we get closer, the structure fully emerges from the ground. A bunker. No—an elevator. A concrete box with a set of glass doors, poking through the center of an island that's now no bigger than a classroom, water just feet away. The doors slide open. The earthquake stops.

"Knowledge accepted," says a hooded figure. "Sufficient credit for entry. Welcome to the Great Library."

15

"What . . ." I stutter. "What's happening?"

The figure removes its hood, revealing the face of a chimpanzee. "The Library operates on a reciprocal information exchange."

Riya protectively pushes her way to the front of the group and stares down the newcomer. "What does that mean, exactly?"

Missi edges in front of Riya. "Thank you, Chief of Security Windsor. But *I'm* the science officer. So, um, yeah. What does that mean?"

The librarian narrows his eyes. "Provide the Library with previously unknown information and, in exchange, you may inquire for yourselves."

Ari catches on. "We tell you stuff. You tell us stuff!"

"Precisely," the librarian says.

Ari nods, working it all out. "You didn't know about us. That we're humans and that some of us escaped the Quarantine. Then I said it out loud."

"For reasons unknown, we have you in our database as a newly awakened species named the Umjerrylochners. But yes, that is accurate. We knew of the execution of the Quarantine on your system. The Minister's data officers regularly offer uploads to the Great Library . . ."

Ari, Becka, and I look at each other. We're not in the Elvid System. But we're not safe either.

"We were not aware," the librarian continues, "that some of you had escaped. That informational offering has granted you access to the Library." He holds out a hand. A paw. Whatever. "This way."

The elevator doors close and we slowly descend beneath the planet's surface. The sunlight dims, replaced by bright artificial lighting inside the elevator. Through the glass: just dirt, at first. Rock. Brown and beige and gray. We begin to move faster. Dark red and orange. Bright, explosive yellow. Faster. Faster. On instinct, we all reach out to steady ourselves. Against the walls. Against each other. But none of us even stumble. The elevator picks up more speed and the planet's inner layers continue zooming past—and we feel nothing. Not a jolt or a jostle.

"Exiting the mantle now," the librarian announces. He reaches into his cloak and pulls out a handful of small foil pouches. "In case anyone is overcome with nausea. It is quite common, I assure you."

"Barf bags," Becka whispers to me. "We're being offered barf bags by a talking monkey."

Missi takes one, just in case.

"Oh," Ari mutters to himself, as we continue to descend. "That reminds me!"

He taps his ring and projects a small holographic chart into the space above his palm. With his free hand, he marks something on the image with his Pencil.

"What's that?" I ask.

"Just a game I'm playing with myself." Ari widens the space between his thumb and forefinger, enlarging the projection for all of us to see.

Ari's Apocalypse Bingo				
~~Alien Invasion~~	~~Robot Uprising~~	Zombies	~~Super-Intelligent Monkeys~~	Particle Accelerator Whoopsy
Pandemic, Natural	Pandemic, Self-Inflicted	Vampires	Ghosts	New Dinosaurs (incl. Godzilla)
Clones	Loss of Technological knowhow/ Reversion to Dark Ages	Free Space!	All Existence Just a Dream/ Simulation	Comic Book Immortal
Bees?	Climate Disaster	Too Much Garbage	Video Games > Real Life	Construction Project Demolition
Religious/ Other	Giant Asteroid	Regular War	Time War	Thumb War

Everyone has questions immediately.

Riya: "Why would clones bring on an apocalypse?"

Ari: "What if they're Hunter clones?"

Riya nods. "Good point."

Missi: "But ghosts aren't real, right?" She spins her head around to ask everyone in the elevator. "RIGHT?!"

Ari shrugs. "Probably not. But are you *sure*?"

Missi shudders.

Becka: "And the vampire apocalypse? Can't you just sprinkle some garlic on them and be done with it?"

"Maybe," Ari answers. "But if vampires make other vampires, it might present a numbers problem. Eventually everyone will be vampires. Not unlike zombies, right?"

"That is correct," the librarian answers gravely.

Ari's eyes go wide. "Wait. What? Which part?"

But the elevator doors open before the librarian can answer, and he ushers us forward. "Welcome to the Great Library."

This place has not been overhyped. It's incredible. A whole city beneath the planet, sparkling below an impossibly large dome. The ceiling sparkles like a bright, starry sky. The path of the Milky Way shimmers and dims. A meteor streaks across the dome. A blindingly colorful nebula whirls into view before disappearing. And below the dome: endless bookshelves, snaking up and down in rows, farther than the eye can see, beyond the horizon. I glance at the shelf closest to me. It's packed with actual paper hardcovers. All the technology in the universe, and these aliens build themselves a library stuffed with books.

Another hooded monkey nods to us as it passes. There must be thousands of them, scattered throughout the library, attending to various aliens. "Who will make the inquiry on your behalf?" our librarian asks.

We all exchange glances before I step forward. It's my turn as captain, after all. "Uh . . . me?" I answer, my voice cracking. I clear my throat and try again. More captainy this time. "Me. I'm in charge."

"What do you wish to learn?"

"The Quarantine," I say. "It sent away our people and we're trying to find anything that might help us figure out where they all went."

The librarian nods. "This way," he tells us, and we follow.

As we walk, Ari taps me on the shoulder and grins, tilting his head at the librarians. Their cloaks. Their hoods. He looks down at my flip-flops, which are making these echoey *smack smack* noises against the cold marble floor every time I take a step.

"Now who looks ridiculous?" Ari says, winking.

The librarian leads us to a shelf in an unremarkable corner of the vast library. He runs a finger along the spines of a dozen books before pulling out a single, tattered hardcover, seemingly at random. It looks ancient, with frayed and yellowing pages.

"This contains the answers you seek," he says, handing me the book.

I open the cover. Flip the pages from end to end. Expecting to understand. But I don't.

"There's nothing here," I say. I turn the book outward to show the others, fanning the pages. "It's blank."

My face feels clammy. My fingers tremble. Even under this enormous dome, it's like the walls are closing in. My claustronervousness again. It's been acting up worse than usual the last couple days, ever since we sealed ourselves in the command pods for those few seconds. I had to clench my eyes shut on the shuttle ride down here, count to three with each deep breath, just like Dr. Hazelwood taught me.

We came all this way for the Great Library to show us . . . nothing. And what's even holding up that dome anyway? I try to catch my breath. Count to three. The dome starts spinning. How far underground are we?! One. Two. Three. Did the book answer my question? One. Two. Three. Did it mean to tell me that—of all the information, in all the galaxy—*nothing* can help us? One. Two. Three. *What's holding up that dome?!*

"The pages are not empty," the librarian says. "They are full. You simply need to unlock what you seek."

But I'm too distracted and terrified to understand.

"Information," Ari explains, squeezing my arm gently. He can always tell when one of my attacks is coming on. "You need to trade."

"But I don't know anything."

"Yes, you do. Everybody knows something. Try talking about yourself."

My head clears a little. Why would the greatest library in the galaxy care about some kid from a nothing moon?

"Um, hello?" I try anyway, speaking into the spine of the book like it's a microphone. "My name is, um, Jacksonville Graham? People call me Jack. And my dad's a teacher? He used to be a scientist." I pause. "I guess he never stopped being a scientist. My mom's a doctor. She lives on Earth. Or, *lived*. Earth is the third planet down from our star. Just in case you didn't know that. Anyway, the Quarantine took my parents away. But a hundred kids escaped on a schoolship named the PSS 118. I was in seventh grade at the time. We've all moved up a year since. Obviously. We have some teachers with us too. The principal's name is Jerry Lochner. He has a middle name, I think, but I don't remember what it is. And he, um, was in the Coast Guard before he went into education? And he likes duck ties?"

I feel silly—until the book sparks, and a sudden electric shock zaps my fingertips. I look down and, sure enough, ink has appeared on one of the pages.

"It *is* magic," Ari breathes.

Magic or not, all my big speech bought us was a single letter, *T*, alone on an otherwise blank page.

"That's it?" I ask.

"Given the offering," the librarian says, "a more than generous response." He starts walking away. "When you are finished, return to your portal. Your island entry point has been restored. And the exterior of your craft has undergone a complimentary cleaning. Be sure to rate and review us on ElvNet!"

"Thanks?" Becka calls out after the librarian. "What do you think ElvNet is?" she asks us.

Missi squints at the bookshelf, sticking her nose into the now-empty space from which the librarian removed our book. "More importantly, what's that?"

Ari peeks into the bookshelf after her. "Huh. A data port?"

Missi raises an eyebrow. "But for what?

Ari narrows his eyes. "I have an idea," he says, holding his communicator ring up to his face. "Ming? Can you hear me? This is Ari. Come in, 118. Repeat: Come in—"

"Yeah," they say. "I can hear you fine. You all okay? We saw the tidal wave and watched the whole thing on our scopes. The shuttle looks okay now, though. I think someone's polishing the hull . . ."

Ari takes his Pencil out of his pocket and begins writing some code in midair, still staring at the shelf. "We're fine, Ming. But listen. There's a data port down here. I don't recognize the input configuration. Shaped like a weird trapezoid. I'm gonna try and synthesize a drive that fits."

"Okay . . ." Ming says back, as confused as the rest of us.

"Okay," Ari echoes, clicking the Pencil. A pinky-sized storage drive materializes in front of us. He plucks it out of the air and tries to wedge it inside the slot in the bookshelf. It doesn't fit. So Ari clicks his Pencil again, dissolves the nanobots, and tries a second time, creating another drive, a bit smaller than the first.

"Bingo," Ari says, pumping his fist. "It's in. Ming, you still there?"

"Reading you loud and clear, Ari."

"Great. The drive I made is also a receiver. Can you read the signature?"

A pause from Ming. So Becka adds, "There's a wide-band signal readout on the right-hand side of the comms command pod."

"I see it," they answer. "Thanks. But there's like ten billion receivers on the planet. Wanna be more specific?"

"Oh yeah," Ari says. "Sorry. I named it Ari-Is-Cool-118."

Ming snorts. "Ha. Okay. Got it."

"Now," Ari says, "upload *everything*."

There's another pause before Ming responds. "As in . . . ?"

"The entire primary databank."

I blink at him. Even before the Quarantine, the 118's main databank had more information in it than we could possibly learn in a lifetime. We're a school. We took history and math and science and art and literature. And with the upgrade, our drives now hold a hundred times what the ship used to know. All of human knowledge. With us wherever we go. And Ari just wants to hand it over.

To a system that communicates with the Minister.

"Captain?" Ming asks me, going over Ari's head in the chain of command.

"You heard him," I say. It's not like I've got any better ideas. "Upload everything."

"Aye, aye," they say back. "It'll take a few minutes."

While we wait, Missi says, "Maybe *you* should be science officer, Ari."

Ari shakes his head. "No way. I get distracted too easily. Besides, I'm on flight duty next, when we're back on the ship. And I'm also on the captain rotation. And . . ."

Missi's face falls.

"*And,*" Ari continues, "you're doing an awesome job. Really. I never would have noticed the drive port in the shelf unless you'd taken the time to look. You pay attention. *That's* why you're science officer."

Missi looks down at the floor but can't help smiling a little. "Thanks."

Suddenly, the book sparks again. Even more than the last time. It's too hot for me to hold. So I lean it against the shelf, propped open. Letters appear on the page, one after the other:

T
h
e
r
e
i
s

"There is," Riya reads out loud.

"There is *what*?!" I yell at the book.

"Ming?" Ari asks into his ring. "Is the upload complete? Is that it?"

"Sorry," they say. "That's everything."

Ari's shoulders slump. "Thanks, Ming. Ari out."

"It was a good try," Missi says.

That can't be it. The library has information that could help us. But even the sum total of all of human knowledge isn't enough for more than two words . . .

"I still love Becka," Ari says out loud, his eyes clenched shut. "Even though we agreed to just be friends. And even though she was, like, kinda mean to me when Hunter took over the ship."

Becka freezes. Riya turns bright red. Missi backs up so far that she smacks into the shelf on the other side of the aisle and a few more empty books fall to the floor.

Ari opens his eyes and gives me a sheepish look. "It's the biggest secret I have," he explains, shrugging.

"I thought . . . Stupid." He turns to Becka. "I'm sorry. I know that we said that—"

"Ari," Becka interrupts. "Look."

The book has given us a whole new word: *another*.

All of human knowledge for two words. Ari's secret, worth almost as much.

"*There is another*," I read, as my heart pounds in my chest. "But another *what?*"

Riya steps forward and speaks to the book. "The last thing I told my mom before the Quarantine was that I hated her. I didn't mean it. But I said it to her on comms after she told me we couldn't afford camp for the summer." She wipes the corners of her eyes with her sleeve. "I didn't know that would be the last thing I said to her before . . . You just don't imagine that . . . I wish I could take it back. I think about it every single day. And I'm so, so sorry."

Missi steps up next. "I was valedictorian last year, right? Because I got straight As and was the perfect student and whatever. But, um." Her voice starts to shake. "You know the science fair projects we did for your dad, Jack? Before everything? I *swore* to Mr. Graham that I'd for sure done mine and uploaded it to ship. I said that the file must have gotten lost or corrupted or something. Um. Well." She takes a shaky breath that's almost a sob. "That was a lie! I choked! I thought that I could measure the curvature of space-time with baking soda and vinegar. But I was . . . I was . . . wrong! And the project was a total bust! So I lied! And he gave me an A anyway because . . . because . . ." She doubles over like she's got a stomach cramp. "He trusted me!"

Riya puts her arm around Missi's shoulders. "It's okay."

Becka sighs, balls her hands into fists, and says, "I know I act tough. And I am. And I know I keep saying that we can do this. And I believe that. But also . . . I really, really miss my parents. I haven't cried about missing them in a while. But it hasn't been *that* long. And I don't miss them any less."

Ari nods. "I really miss my parents too."

Missi and Riya chime in. "Me too," they both say.

I think about my mom and dad. One of them left our family for a new life halfway across the solar system. The other literally brought on the end of the world. I've been so mad at them, so much, over this past year. And I'd do anything to see them again. Even for a minute. "Me too," I echo.

The book sparks a third time, giving up another word.

Ship.

"There is another ship," I read.

"Another *human* ship?" Ari asks excitedly. "That escaped the Quarantine?"

"Could be an alien ship," Missi suggests. "But there must be countless alien ships. Why would this one be special?"

We have to be careful with our questions. We only have so much information to give in return. "What's the ship called?" I ask the book. "And how can we find it?"

But the book stays silent.

I wrack my brain for something else to offer. I don't just miss my parents. I miss *everything* about my old life. Regular school. My cramped apartment in our crowded five-story walk-up housing pod on Ganymede. The drip-drip shower pressure from all the water rationing. Even the ants that started creeping into our pod after an infested supply shipment from Earth somehow made it past the customs inspection. I miss those ants. But realizing that "the terraforming is always greener on the other side" doesn't seem like a big enough secret for the Great Library of Wyzardia.

Nothing about my life has ever been interesting enough, special enough. We've uploaded everything the 118 knows. Everything *humanity* knows. We have no secrets left. Nothing worthwhile that the library doesn't already know.

Unless . . .

I look at Ari and Becka and can't believe it hasn't occurred to them yet. Or maybe it has. Maybe they're just not willing to trade that particular bit of information. A secret even the Minister doesn't know. A secret she's already tried to squeeze out of us.

I shouldn't do it. We already know this place isn't safe from the Elvidians. And if the Minister finds out . . .

He's done so much to help us. If I reveal his identity to the library, and the library reveals it to the Minister, we'll lose our only friend in the galaxy, and I'll have betrayed someone who's been trying to do the right thing.

I stare at the book: *There is another ship.*

The right thing.

It feels wrong. In a lot of ways, it *is* wrong. But here and now, there's no perfect choice.

"Whatever it takes?" I ask Ari and Becka. To get our people home. To find my parents and everyone else the Quarantine sent away. And hey, maybe it won't get back to the Minister? Maybe what happens in the library stays in the library?

I don't know.

And it doesn't matter.

Ari and Becka understand what I mean. I can see it in their faces. "Whatever it takes," Becka agrees, and Ari nods.

I take a deep breath. "Bale Kontra betrayed the Minister," I tell the book. "He's been helping us humans all along."

This time, the book practically explodes. Bolts of electricity jump off the page. A puff of smoke blasts upward. The book jumps off the shelf and lands, still open, at Ari's feet.

I cough and wave away the smoke. "So?" I ask Ari, as he picks up the book and stares at its pages. "What does it say?"

Like a failed rocket, Ari's face blasts off, thrilled—then crashes down, devastated. He turns the book around so we can all see. "The ship is called the Poplar," he reads, his voice cracking. I wonder if that's just the closest translation, or if there actually are poplar trees all over the galaxy. But Ari's not finished.

"Its transponder was last registered at these coordinates . . . on the surface of Elvid IX."

Elvid IX.

Home of the Minister.

16

"Here's the thing," I say. I'm standing at the front of the mess hall, leading an assembly. Becka's with me, and Ari's flying the ship. After reboarding, we engaged the light speed engine and headed straight for the massive, ringed planet that is Elvid IX.

We're back. At the edge of a boundary only the three of us have crossed before—a boundary I'd hoped to never cross again. "The planet is surrounded by something the Elvidians call Orientation."

Missi's hand shoots up.

"Yeah, Missi?"

"But what *is* Orientation?"

I blink at her. "Um, thanks, Missi. I was about to explain that. Orientation is a . . . mind game. I don't know how else to describe it. Once Ari takes us through the barrier, we'll be hit with this blue light. One second, you'll be sitting here. The next second . . ." I snap my fingers. "You'll be somewhere else."

Missi raises her hand again.

"*Yes,* Missi?"

"But *where* will we be?"

Becka steps in. "You'll be right here. We think. Only your mind will be inside Orientation."

"It's a simulation," I explain. "To try and trick you into loving the Minister."

A few kids laugh. Because I guess it sounds ridiculous. But it's not.

I crane my neck to look at Hunter, Madison, and Kingston in the way back. We've gathered the prisoners here too—under Chief of Security Riya Windsor's watchful guard, of course. She didn't want to let them out of the brig, but I overruled her. Even they deserve to be prepared.

Again, Missi raises her hand. "What did *you* see, last time?"

Becka and I look at each other. She has only the vaguest idea of what I saw: Her and Ari, together, bullying me into changing my mind about the Minister. And Becka? She's been even quieter about what she went through. All I know is that it involved a scenario where Diana was in danger and Becka could only save her sister with the Minister's help.

"Everybody sees something different," Becka says, glancing at Diana and then looking away. "And whatever it is, it isn't fun."

"Just remember," I say, "it's not real."

Some nods. Becka and I sit down and buckle up.

"Ari," I say over the comms, "Take us in."

"Aye, aye," he says in a shaky voice.

We move forward and receive our first message from that creepy mind-voice that I did *not* miss.

"**CHECKPOINT**," it says, then: "**NON-INDIG-INOUS LIFE-FORMS DETECTED.**"

The crowd is murmuring. Panicking.

"It's okay," I tell them. Tell myself.

From the across the room, a wave of blue light washes through the walls and rushes toward us, hitting the kids in the back of the mess hall first, scanning Becka and me last.

"**ASSESSMENT COMPLETE**," the voice says. "**COMMENCING ORIENTATION.**"

Becka looks at me. "Here we—"

Pop.

***

"—go."

We rematerialize on a long line surrounded by who-knows-how-many other lines. We're waiting our turn to pass through the edges of this cloud-like space, into the dream (slash nightmare) that is Orientation. We shuffle forward. The Elvidian clerks at the front shout, "Next!" every few seconds. And we pass the time by gawking at all the aliens in here.

I see some rhinogoats. Some Statues of Liberty. And some species I've never encountered before: a group of snail creatures with sparkly shells; a couple of floating—I don't know—zebra pterodactyls? (zebradactyls?); and several aliens who look (and waddle) exactly like human toddlers, except they're dressed in business suits and talk like grumpy, middle-aged men.

"How's the job?" one baby says to another, toddling forward in line.

The second baby shrugs. "Another day, another credit. Catch the big game last night?"

Eventually—"Next!"—it's my turn.

I walk up to the booth at the front of our line. "Distrusting, level three," the Elvidian guard says, chomping down on some gum. "Approval-seeking, level six. Abandonment-fearing, level five. Long live the—"

"Yeah, yeah," I say to him, walking into the mist. "Long live the Minister. Let's get this over with."

* * *

It takes a moment for my eyes to adjust. However bright the Orientation waystation was, this place is much brighter.

This place.

Blue skies visible through glass. An enormous floor-to-ceiling window. My vision focuses, and I take in the sprawling city: We're at the foot of a crystal-clear bay, sparkling in the sunlight. About ten blocks ahead, a golden dome sticks up out of the skyline. Beyond that, an enormous orange bridge, and green mountains in the background.

"Welcome to San Francisco," she says from behind me. I turn, and my mom looks exactly as I remember her. Which I guess makes sense, given that this whole thing is in my mind. Reddish-blondish hair. Skin like mine, pale and freckly. Crinkles around her nose whenever she smiles or frowns. "What do you think?"

I take in the apartment, which—I'm trying to remember—have I ever seen? Maybe in pictures or the rare video call. It's enormous. Ten times the size of mine and my dad's place on Ganymede, easy. Was her real apartment this big? Or is this just how I always imagined it? My very first thought is: She had this much room and still didn't invite me to visit? I could've stayed for a week and never run into her!

Which I know is a thought that makes no sense because, again, not real.

It's a corner apartment, with windows that wrap around two whole walls of the living room. There's a kitchen and dining room behind her and a winding hallway—leading to bedrooms, I guess—even farther back. Everything's so bright and colorful. Splashes of pink, purple, and green. Dark blue furniture on white carpeting. A whole wall of digital paper displaying the other side of the city, as if the room actually has windows on three sides instead of just two. Photographs on every flat surface: My mom in front of the Eiffel Tower. My mom at the foot of the Pyramids at Giza. My mom after a hike up Olympus Mons in the Martian Neutral Zone—very touristy.

(Did she really go to all those places?)

(I can't believe she went without me!)

(Stop it, Jack! This is all in your head.)

"It's nice," I say, planting my feet. "But it isn't real."

My mom tilts her head and I wait for the explosion. Last time, when I pushed back against fake Orientation Becka and Orientation Ari, things got . . . weird. My mom just laughs; and it feels like fresh air blowing in through the windows. Goosebumps on my skin. She isn't real. But she *feels* real. "I know that, Jackie." She holds out her arms. "Doesn't mean we can't enjoy ourselves a little, though, right?"

My jaw drops open. "Wait. You know you're not real?"

She shrugs. "I mean, what's real? Are *you* real?"

Before I can answer, she interrupts, "Are you sure?" She waves her hands around in that way I've seen her do a thousand times, like she's gently swatting away a swarm of butterflies. "Sorry. I didn't mean to get philosophical. To answer your question, yes, I know I'm not real. Not as real as you."

"I . . . I don't understand."

She sits down on the couch and pats the cushion next to her. "Sit, Jackie. Please."

I know, I know, I *know*, it's not her. But what else am I supposed to do?

I sit down on the other end of the couch. I'm not getting any closer to her. Not yet. "Do you know why you're here?" she asks.

"Because the Minister is an evil loser who needs everyone to love her?"

My Orientation mom flinches when I say the word "loser."

"Because," she corrects, "you're about to enter the orbit of one of the greatest planets in all the civilized galaxy. Because the Minister *built* that planet. And because she deserves credit for her work. For advancing all of us. For keeping us safe."

"Aha," I say, rolling my eyes. "So this is the part where I tell you that I'll never love the Minister and you freak out on me, right? Then we start this whole thing over?"

She laughs again. A familiar-to-my-core laugh. Tears pool in my eyes, and my brain flashes with a memory of her crouching down inside the communal garden near our housing pod on Ganymede, laughing at some joke my dad told. I shake the memory away. Wipe away the tears.

That was real. This isn't.

This. Isn't.

"Not to get philosophical again," my fake simulation mom says. "But that memory isn't real either. With the flowers. It's something that happened, *maybe*. Like you remember it, *maybe*. Or maybe it happened differently. Maybe it didn't happen at all and you only *think* it did. That exact moment exists nowhere but inside your own mind. Just neurons and synapses in your brain." She smiles. "Just like me."

"Get out of my head," is all I can say.

Another laugh. It makes my me feel fuzzy. Dizzy. "We're both in your head now, sweetie," she says, scooting toward me. "And we're not resetting. Not this time."

"What do you mean?"

"You asked whether we'd be starting over again. I'm just answering your question. We're not resetting. Whatever you went through last time . . ." She pauses and tilts her head, reading my mind again. "I see. How unpleasant. It won't be like that. The algorithm is different every time, and *this time*"—she scoots closer again— "it's going to be me and you, as long as it takes."

"As long as it takes," I repeat, the words terrifying me.

But not completely.

"I'm so glad you understand." She smiles and opens her palm, triggering a row of holographic images that fly out of her ring. She swats in the air and scrolls until she gets to what looks like a menu for some salad place. "Should we order dinner? I was thinking takeout. This place gets the freshest veggies, locally printed. You've had a long day and must be hungry."

Thing is, I *am* hungry.

So we get dinner. And it's okay. Not great, not terrible. Just a normal dinner with my imaginary mom. We chat about Ganymede and San Francisco. We play a little Neptune Attacks 3, which hasn't even come out in real life yet! And in this weird mind simulation, the series *finally* has a decent one-player campaign mode. She tells me about work. I tell her a bit about how Dad's doing. About school. She reminds me that classes start tomorrow, which is obviously nonsense, so I ignore her.

Until she says goodnight and shows me to my room, and—again, what else am I supposed to do?—I go to sleep and wake up and . . . go to school. She's enrolled me in this fancy charter school a few streets over where—*what else am I supposed to do?*—I spend the next day, which turns into the next week, which turns into the next month.

I make imaginary friends. (Sia Grange, who's the best dodgeball player I've ever seen. And Draper Yazoo, who *tripled* the nanobot capacity of my Pencil. Don't tell Becka and Ari.) I annoy imaginary teachers. (Turns out, Principal Parrish does not appreciate being told that he "isn't real.") I do imaginary homework. (And *still* can't manage to get As, but whatever.)

Only my mom seems to know she's part of a simulation. My mom and me, I mean. And it gets tiring to talk about it all the time. So we talk about other things. Everything. A good listener is a good listener, even when she's an evil simulation of your mother designed to brainwash you into loving an alien queen.

Sometimes, she even apologizes for leaving Dad and me. She tells us that she just wasn't cut out to be a good parent on a small moon. And that she would've been an even worse parent if she'd taken me with her. But that she still wishes there'd been another way. *Look at these pictures, these photo albums, of the three of us together. Look at us smiling. You were so happy. We could be happy like that again. Things are already better, aren't they? Aren't you happy?*

I am. Right? I *feel* happy. And what's real, anyway? Just neurons and synapses. Her apologies are so sincere. And she tells me that she and Dad wouldn't have had to split up . . . if only I'd done the right thing. If only I'd loved the Minister more. Then Dad and I could've come to Earth with her. We could have all stayed together. We still can. If only I love the Minister. Which I *know* isn't quite right—but can't remember why.

***

At first, I assume that my mom was lying—that we're starting over after all. But no. We're back. I'm back. Onboard the 118, right where I was sitting before Orientation began.

I look behind me at the control panel on the wall. A whopping twenty seconds have passed in the real world, and we've all woken up. Some kids are crying. Others are staring straight ahead, silent. Albi Butler throws up onto his sneakers.

Becka quickly gets on internal comms, almost tripping over her chair and falling to the floor. "Ari?" she asks. "You all right? Ari?"

No answer.

"Ari?!"

"Yeah," he says through the speaker. "I'm fine. Well, maybe not fine. But . . . you know. We're through and I'm taking us down to the surface. Can we *please* never do that again?"

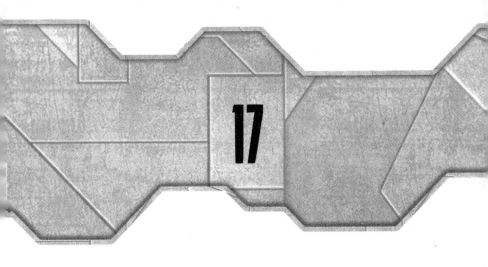

17

"Are you sure this is it?" I ask Ari.

We're lying on our stomachs in the dirt, staring down at the valley below. Peering through high-powered binoculars that we brought from the ship. And breathing through oxygen masks—because while the natural atmosphere is technically breathable, Elvid IX has been hopelessly poisoned by pollution from the planet's nearly endless city. Even down here, in a rare pocket of empty desert, the air is hazy with smog.

Ari nods and adjusts the zoom on his binoculars, focusing on the quiet tent village in the valley. "I'm sure. The last registered public hit for the Poplar's transponder was right there."

It's only the three of us on this expedition. It seemed more dangerous than the mission to Wyzardia. So this time, Riya and Missi stayed with Ming onboard the 118, which we parked a couple miles away, closer to the city. If something happens to us, everyone else will be in good hands. They'll be able to keep going.

Also, it's kind of nice. "The dream team," Ari keeps calling us.

The mission is simple. Reconnaissance only. The Poplar should be here, somewhere. According to the public ship registry, which we were able to access from low orbit, its transponder hasn't pinged in years. Which at least tells us that the ship probably didn't come from our home system.

"Over there." Ari points to a row of identical, narrow groundcraft behind the tents, lining one of the valley walls.

"Are those ships?" asks Becka doubtfully.

I zoom in as far as I can. "Can't tell from this distance. We'll need to get a closer look."

Becka adjusts her binoculars. "Heads up, we've got locals on the move."

The suns are beginning to rise and, with them, the village is waking up. Aliens of all kinds are streaming out of dirt-stained tents, lining up behind uniformed Elvidians shouting orders I can't hear. I shift my binoculars to the sign posted by the nearest cave entrance and filter the alien words through the translation software in my digital contacts: "FIRST ELVIDIAN MINES (Sector 15)."

It's some kind of work camp. And the first shift is about to start.

"That's a lot of Elvidians," Ari whispers, whistling to himself.

I nod. "Hopefully, they'll all go into the cave. Then we can have a look around."

With a gasp, Ari points down at the cluster of aliens closest to the cliffside—and us. They're dressed in thick jumpsuits, breathing through small rectangular devices no bigger than harmonicas. They're putting on gear: helmets, harnesses, belts. And a few are drinking something that my mind wants to think is coffee or tea, even though its steam is blue. These aliens are big. Most of them are seven or eight feet tall, although there's a small one in the mix too. A kid, maybe. They've got round ears and sharp teeth. And they're covered from head to toe in yellow hair, thicker around their necks and heads.

"Magnificent," Ari marvels. "It's a whole race of hamster people."

Becka laughs. "No it's not!"

"Ari," I say, "they're clearly a race of *lion* people."

Becka nods. "Totally."

Ari looks again through the binoculars. "They look like hamster people to me."

"They're also leaving," Becka notes, standing up. She's right. All the aliens are forming lines and marching toward the mouth of the cave.

I lower my binoculars. "Let's go."

We hike down the shallowest ridge, into the valley below, and walk toward the vehicles.

"I think they're hoverbikes of some kind," I say as we get closer. "See the open-air seating? Enough for one person, maybe two. Not meant for space. I doubt that's what the library was talking about."

They're beat-up and rusty. Most of them are caked with dust.

"So not the Poplar," Becka says, writing *Wash Me* with her finger on the side of the closest bike.

"But if the Poplar's not here," Ari says, "how will we ever find it?"

Fair question. The trail goes cold here. And if we have to search this whole planet for one ship, well, it's gonna be like trying to find an asteroid in the belt.

Someone huffs out of a nearby tent. It's a rhinogoat, breathing the air somehow, and lugging an enormous loop of ropes.

"Um, excuse me!" Ari calls.

"Shhh," I say. "Reconnaissance only, remember?"

The rhinogoat waves off Ari and picks up the pace. "I'm late!"

"Have you heard of the Poplar?" Ari yells after him anyway. "It's a ship! Ever seen it?"

"I'm late!" the rhinogoat repeats, ducking between two tents and out of sight.

Off to the side, though, someone shouts, "Hey, you!"

We turn. The smaller lion-alien we spotted earlier has popped out of a tent. The alien takes one step toward us, shaking a long mane of hair, and says, "Did you say the Poplar?"

Becka, Ari, and I look at each other.

"Yeah," I tell the alien—the a*lion*?—whose eyes suddenly go wide with fear. "It's a ship we're looking for. Have you seen it?"

In response, the alion bolts away.

We follow—through a row of tents, across the mouth of the mining cave. We lose ground with every second, slower on our two human legs than the alion is on its all-fours sprint.

"Wait!" Ari shouts as we try to keep up. "We come in peace! I have a pet hamster at home!"

The alion throws a leg over one of the hoverbikes and kicks it into ignition with two taps of its heels. The bike snaps upward, hovering a few inches off the ground. The alion speeds away into the open desert, shouting, "Please! For the love of the Great Old Ones, just leave me alone!"

Frustrated, I punch the nearest rock face. "We'll never catch up now!"

Becka pushes past me. "Not if I have anything to say about it."

She hops on another bike and imitates the alien's *kick-kick* motion. The vehicle beneath her roars to life. "You coming?"

Ari breaks into a wide grin.

"One second," he says, writing out a word or two with his Pencil. Ari clicks, and three floating helmets appear in the air. He tosses one to me and one to Becka. Plunks the third onto his own head. "Safety first!"

Becka straps on her helmet and takes off in pursuit.

Ari moves toward another dingy hoverbike. "This one. You drive. I have an idea."

There's no time to waste. Becka's already speeding ahead. I jump onto the bike and kick it into gear. Ari hops on behind me, linking his arms around my torso.

"Here we go!" I yell, feeling for the controls and hoping my instincts are right.

I rev the engines. Twist the handlebars. And zoom—backward. We plow straight through the closest tent, which collapses around us.

"Other way!" Ari shouts.

I roll my eyes and restart the bike in the right direction. "You think?"

We take off into the desert.

I spot Becka's bike in the distance. She's catching up to the alion, who's trying to shake the tail by zipping around in sharp figure eights, one after the other. As Ari and I speed closer, Becka pulls up alongside the alion and tries to cut them off. But the alion speeds past, nicking the front of Becka's bike, which careens out of control. Becka leaps off at the last second—landing in a sand dune—and her bike plunges into a nearby boulder, exploding into a ball of flame.

I feel Ari's whole body flinch, but Becka's okay. "Keep going!" she calls to us, shaking sand out of her hair as we pass.

I twist the handlebars again, pushing the bike as fast

as it'll go. Behind me, Ari's fidgeting with something. I can't tell what.

We're gaining. But the alion isn't the only thing that's getting closer. This pocket of desert is only a few miles across. The rest of Elvid IX is—

"The city!" Ari shouts.

"I see it!"

Rising up in the distance. Impossibly tall buildings crammed together along every inch of the horizon. Pyramids and smokestacks cluttering the skyline. And closer to eye level, a huge concrete wall, bordering the desert on all sides. The alion's heading right for it.

"Try that!" Ari points to an indicator light on the hoverbike. Even with my translator contacts, I can't read all the controls. The words buzz in and out of focus. But if Ari says to try it . . . I press the button.

The hoverbike shudders—I take a heartbeat to glance behind me—and a rocket booster unfurls from the back of the vehicle. It explodes outward. And we speed up.

I pump a fist, glad the alien doesn't seem to know this trick. "Now we're talk—"

Something's not right. We pass over a small dune, and the fire from the rocket booster kicks up so much sand that—

"I can't see!" I scream at Ari, sand invading my mouth and eyes.

"THE MINISTER WARNS YOU TO BE VIG-ILANT AGAINST CRIMINALS AND OTHER

MISCREANTS. REPORT SUSPICIOUS BEHAV-
IOR TO . . .”

The voice is coming from a billboard up ahead. The
Minister's half-3D image, projecting out from the closest stretch of border wall. We must've tripped a sensor.
For a moment, the light from the hologram cuts through
the swirl of sand, reflecting off the metal hull of the
other bike. It's still ahead of us. We're still gaining. Until
the alion turns sharply, flying parallel to the city walls—
which I could have sworn were farther away.

"Look out!" Ari screams into my ear.

I try to brake. But it's too late. The wall is directly in
front of us. I close my eyes. And we *crash*—

Into a particle shield, protecting the wall. Instead of
exploding against the concrete, our hoverbike bounces
off the shield like a rubber ball and we hurtle up and
away in an out-of-control spin. My eyes are open now.
Ari and I are both screaming. As we arc through the
smoky sky, the hoverbike tech recalibrates and we level
out, booster off but still riding at full speed.

Inches behind the alion.

When the alion turns around, I can see their eyes,
widened in shock at how close we've gotten.

"Gotcha!" Ari shouts, and I feel him move his arm.
Maybe to try and grab hold of the other bike. Maybe to
grab the alion. But Ari only catches air.

That's when I see them all. Hoverbikes. Cars. Freighter-
sized, self-driving delivery hovertrucks. Streaking back and

forth across the desert, right in front of us. Traffic zooming in and out of a tunnel leading underneath the wall.

"Pull up!" Ari screams.

"We're on a bike!" I shout back. "That's not a thing!"

"So stop!"

"It's too late!"

We follow the alien bike into a dozen lanes of traffic. Swerving around cars. Barely missing a collision with a honking hovertruck. I blink and there's another truck. And another. There's not enough room!

One truck—built like a sharp-angled train locomotive—clips the front of our bike, slicing its nose clean off. I lose control. We're spinning . . .

And suddenly—we're clear of it all, sliding into the empty desert, surfing the sand. Gradually we come to a stop. Our hoverbike is toast. The alion is far ahead, and getting farther.

* * *

By the time we hike back to the valley where we first saw the alien, Becka's already there. Slumped on the ground. Chin in her hands.

"I can't believe we lost the trail," she says without looking up.

I smile. "Actually . . ."

I let Ari say the rest. He gestures toward the mouth of the mining cave. "The hamsterite came back here.

Went underground about fifteen minutes ago."

Becka jumps up and follows us toward the entrance. "How do you know?"

The cave is enormous, branching off into at least thirty separate tunnels that lead deep beneath the planetary surface. "Because," Ari answers, tossing up a hologram from his ring, "I'm tracking them."

Four dots appear on the hologram: three clustered close together at one end, unmoving, and one snaking through passageways that materialize on the map as the dot moves.

"I put the finishing touches on my Pencil tracking program," Ari explains. "The code isn't pretty, but it should do the trick. I borrowed some of the strings from the *HAMSTER MECH* app, which already had built-in nav tracking in case Doctor Shrew ever goes too far. Anyway, we got close enough to the alien at one point that the tracker was easy to throw onto their jumpsuit. I made it sticky, too. Like those lights we used on the last day of seventh grade."

I'm grinning from ear to ear. Ari explained all this to me on our walk. And judging by how Becka's staring at him, she's just as delighted as I am.

"What?" Ari asks defensively. "Did I do something wrong?"

Becka smirks. "Never." She points toward the tunnel entrance that matches the alien's position on Ari's map. "Shall we?"

ARI'S LOG: DAY 183

What do you think Becka meant by, "Never"? Was she being sarcastic? Aren't I "the weak one"? Maybe I'm overthinking it. I'm definitely not <u>underthinking</u> it. But it's only been a few days since I confessed my undying love for her in front of a bunch of our friends and the galaxy's central library system. So, you know, I've had kind of <u>a week</u>.

Focus, Ari. Focus. There's a whole species of hamster aliens! Yellowish/brownish fur? Check. Black eyes as dark as the cosmic void? Double-check. Little pink finger-paws so cute you could faint? Check, check, check. If that doesn't describe a hamster-person, tell me what does. Besides, I'd see to see a lion drive a hoverbike like <u>that</u>. Just saying. Hamsters are natural escape artists! Sure, "alion" makes a good pun. Doesn't mean they actually look like lions. This is my professional opinion, as the galaxy's foremost authority on hamsters. (And with all the other humans disappeared, this might be literally true.)

Whoops. Got distracted again. Sorry. So there we were in the mines, following Starlee's signal deeper into the tunnels. (Wait, did we not talk about how her name is Starlee? Sorry. SUPER TINY SPOILER ALERT: The name of the alien we were chasing is Starlee, pronouns she/her.)

We had to sneak past all these other aliens chipping away at the walls. Not to mention the Elvidians watching them from the shadows—threatening them, keeping them on task. Luckily, the mines were noisy and dark. Perfect for sneaking, with all the yelling and the mining and whatnot. The miners collect chunks of silvery rock into hexagonal boxes that are constantly compressing what's inside. Like portable mini trash compactors. Their chik chik sound gives the caves a kind of a rhythm. Jack and I started beatboxing to the alien machines, but Becka shushed us. She said it's because we were drawing too much attention to ourselves. But we all know it's because Jack and I are better beatboxers than she is. (Please don't tell her I said that.)

We followed Starlee for hours, till it had to be way past nightfall. But there's no natural light down there, so who knows. I don't think the miners are working 9 to 5. And when the tunnel finally opened up into a larger cavern, where Starlee and the other hamster people were camped—and asleep—we took the opportunity to get a little rest too.

ARI'S LOG: DAY 184

Naturally, they didn't wake us up until AFTER they tied up our wrists and chained our legs to a giant bolder. "Who are you?" one them said. There were maybe six or seven Hamsterites gathered around us. Starlee was holding hands with two of them. Her moms, she later told us.

Jack spoke up, because he was the captain: "Um, yeah, hi. My name is Jack. And these are my friends Becka and Ari. We're here looking for a ship? It's called the Poplar. Or it was. Once."

As soon as Jack mentioned the Poplar, I knew we were in the right place. You could see it on their faces. I'm also an expert at reading hamster. One of Starlee's moms clutched a chain around her neck, holding what looked like a small orange-gold whistle. "Why did you follow our daughter down here?"

"While we were asking around, she seemed to recognize the name of the ship," Jack explained.

Starlee's moms glared at her. We'd gotten her in trouble. "I didn't mean to give anything away," she said. "I was just surprised."

"Tell me why you want to know about the Poplar," said the angrier mom—the one with the necklace. She put a hand on her belt and pulled what looked like a laser weapon.

Jack—being the boss that he is—took a deep breath and went for it: "Our solar system was attacked by an Elvidian teleportation weapon called the Quarantine. Only a few of us made it out, and we're looking for everyone else. But we don't know where to go or what to do. We learned about the Poplar from the Great Library in the Wyzard System. We still don't know what it has to do with all this. But we figure maybe its crew knows something. Maybe they can help us."

"And we have celery!" I tried. But I'm guessing the aliens have plenty of celery in their tent anyway, because they didn't seem tempted. Instead, Starlee's moms looked at each other. One said, "Sorry, kid." And they stunned us unconscious with their blasters.

ARI'S LOG: FLASHBACK

This seems like as good a time as any to tell you about the day I got Doctor Shrew. It was the summer between sixth and seventh grade. Only a few days after the untimely demise of our twenty-four-year-old orange tabby cat, Lawrence Tangerine, Esq. Dad got Larry before he met Abba. And they kept him—even though Abba was super allergic and the neighborhood air recyclers weren't great at filtering out cat hair except for like one day a month, right after maintenance inspections. (There was also a moonwide brownout one spring break, which cut power to the sector's gravitometric field generators for maybe four five seconds. We were cleaning kitty litter out of the carpet for weeks.)

Anyway, if you didn't know him, you probably would've thought that Larry wasn't the most social of creatures. For example, he never (1) played with me, (2) slept in my bed, (3) ate or drank when I was around, or (4) interacted with me in any significant way. But I could tell he was just playing it cool. I loved the guy. When he died, I was DEVASTATED. Cried alone in my room for days. Just like Larry would have wanted. And the next week, when Abba brought Doctor Shrew home from the animal shelter in the Busiris Commercial District, I couldn't even look at him and swore I'd never love again.

Just goes to show: You never know.

ARI'S LOG: DAY 185

They must have dragged us out of the mine. Because we woke up inside their desert tent, surrounded by the same group of Hamsterians. (Did you like "Hamsterites" better? I'm still working through the options.)

"Hi," Starlee said to us. "I'm Starlee. Sorry my moms tied you up."

"It's okay," I told her. "We kinda get captured a lot."

She giggled at my joke. And I laughed at her laughing. Then Becka glared at me, because I guess she didn't think I should be getting friendly with our captors. Which isn't a terrible point. But, you know, Hamsterites!

"So . . . when're you letting us go?" I asked.

Starlee didn't have time to answer. One of her moms walked over and said, "Who else knows you're here?"

"No one," Becka said.

But I didn't think that was the safest answer, given all the movies I'd seen about getting kidnapped, so I added, "Except the rest of our ship. They know. And they'll come looking for us."

The aliens all looked at each other, and one of Starlee's moms cut open our ropes. "Listen to me very carefully," she said. "If you know what's good for you, you'll stop asking questions that will only cause trouble. And not just for you. The Quarantine hit our people too."

I couldn't help interrupting with, "And your people are called what, exactly?"

But she ignored me. "Like you, a few of us managed to escape before the countdown ended. Like you, we're the last of our kind. And like you, we went poking our snouts where they didn't belong. Not only did we fail to rescue our people, but we lost what little we had left. Our ship. Our freedom. Everything." She pulled open the entrance to the tent, her paws shaking. "You can't beat the Minister. If you're playing her game, she's already won. Leave. Now. If we see you again, we will tell the Elvidians. And then that'll be two lost peoples forced to work the mines forever."

19

"So they seemed nice," Ari says as we sit together in the mess hall, trying to figure out what to do next.

"They were horrible," Becka argues. "They tied us up and threatened us."

Ari shrugs. "They were protecting themselves. They've been through a lot."

"*We've* been through a lot," Becka says. "And we don't threaten people."

Ari raises an eyebrow. "Except that time last year when we tied up an Elvidian soldier and used Doctor Shrew to threaten him with being eaten." Ari tosses Doctor Shrew a stalk of celery. The hamster is circling the room in his mech suit, which makes this wheezing *see-zee* sound every time he takes a step. As the celery flies toward him, Doctor Shrew jumps like fifteen feet in the air to catch it. "And also last week, when we tried to trick those robots into thinking Jack had a bomb? And again when . . ."

"Okay!" Becka puts up her hands. "But it's not the same, and you know it. We never go after someone who's less powerful than we are. We only do what we have to do when someone else is trying to hurt *us*."

"Yeah, but the Hamsteroids couldn't be sure that we wouldn't hurt them."

"I can't believe you right now. Taking their side."

"What's that supposed to mean? Because I'm so *gullible*?"

"I've apologized for saying that a hundred times already."

I zone out, replaying the gist of the alion's speech in my head. How they tried to find their people. How—by trying—they lost what little they had left.

". . . can't understand why you'd defend those . . ."

". . . seem like perfectly nice sentient hamsters to me . . ."

". . . given us absolutely no reason to trust them . . ."

". . . sometimes have to have faith that people are who they say they are . . ."

"I'm taking a walk," I announce. Becka and Ari are too busy arguing to notice.

It's late. Most of the students are asleep in their dorms. I hear the *bounce-bounce* of a basketball, so I guess a few kids are playing in the gym. Gena and Cal are doing a great job keeping all the others in line. I know they've got a curfew going, with a rotating schedule of "late night allowances." The lights are on in the library too.

I think Riya's studying a manual on the ship's boarding countermeasures. She waves at me through the window as I pass.

We've finally got 118 running like clockwork. Too bad we've got nowhere to go.

I head to Classroom 3, where we've still got Hunter locked up. Riya's disabled all internal controls and comms. And Ari and Missi worked together on a special biometric bolt to keep the door sealed. If this side of the school is the brig, Classroom 3 is maximum security.

Antonio Gomez-Perez is on watch. He's only a sixth grader, and I can't help but wonder if he's up to the task.

Antonio nods at me and I nod back. "Let me in?" I say.

"Aye, aye, Captain," Antonio says, saluting. Very professional. I've got to stop doubting people. But can you blame me? The teachers let us down. Half the school revolted. And the spy is still out there, somewhere. Even Becka and Ari are having a hard time getting along.

Antonio opens the door and locks it behind me.

"Come to gloat?" Hunter grumbles. He's lying on the floor in the center of the room, staring up at the ceiling. We removed the furniture, the school supplies, even the posters. Anything not nailed down that Hunter could use to try and escape. "I don't have much to offer you."

I sit down on the floor a few feet away from him. "Did you spy for the Minister?"

He snorts, eyes still on the ceiling. "I already told Riya. *No.* I thought the mission was stupid, but that doesn't mean I'm on her side."

It's the same answer he's been giving since we retook the ship. And I believe him. I've always believed him. But I couldn't help thinking that if we could at least answer this question, maybe we could start answering the other ones too.

"Is that it?" Hunter says, finally turning his head to look at me. "Captain Graham's brilliant strategy on display! Asking the same questions over and over!"

Hunter's as pleasant as always.

"Why are you so angry all the time?" I ask him. "And don't tell me it's because of the Quarantine. You've obviously been angry for a lot longer than we've been out here."

He sits up. "Isn't it obvious? I'm angry because everything's terrible. And it's all the same. It's always been the same. Being on this ship. Getting attacked by freaking aliens. It's us drawing the short straw over and over and over. Our families live—*lived*—on Ganymede, because they couldn't afford a better moon. We got sent to the PSS 118 because someone thinks it's funny to send kids from poor neighborhoods to schoolships that literally can't be used for anything else anymore. And now, here we are." He lies back down. "Living the dream."

"But we're *lucky*," I tell him. "We didn't get captured by the Quarantine. We're still here. We're still fighting."

He shakes his head. "That's the worst luck of all. If we'd been taken, at least we'd finally be off this ship. At least we'd be with our families. . ." He stops short. "At least we wouldn't be so alone."

I'm frozen. No idea what to say. Whether to try to make him feel better—whether to try to make *myself* feel better—or whether to stop trying.

We're stuck. Out of ideas. Turning on each other. You can only take life one step at a time for so long. At some point, the road ends and there's no place left to go.

I think about my mom and dad. Are they okay, wherever they are? I imagine them finding each other somewhere. Scared for me, not knowing where I am.

"Yeah," Hunter says, nodding at my expression. "*That's* why I'm so angry."

"AHEM," the ship says. "*I DON'T MEAN TO INTERRUPT THIS . . . WHATEVER THIS IS. BUT JACK, YOUR PRESENCE IS REQUESTED IN THE MESS HALL. YOU'D BETTER GET THERE QUICK.*"

"Hooray," Hunter says flatly. "Better get going. I bet the solution to all our problems is just around the corner."

20

Lost in my head, I almost pass the entrance to the mess hall on my way back through the corridor. But the raised voices bring me back. *Three* voices. I spin around and press my hand to the door panel.

"Put it down, Becka!" Ari begs as the doors slide open. "She's not going to hurt us!"

"I'm supposed to believe that?" Becka says. She's pointing her blaster at Starlee.

And Starlee is pointing one of her own right back at Becka.

"How'd you get onboard?" I demand.

"Uh, the front door was unlocked."

I glare at Ari. "You were supposed to lock the main hatch behind us before we left the planet!"

Ari glares right back. "I thought *you* were supposed to lock the main hatch!"

"Riya is not going to be happy when she hears about this security breach," Becka says.

"Look, I'm here to help," Starlee insists.

I immediately pull my own blaster out of its holster and aim it at the alion. "Here to help *how*, exactly? By leading us on another wild meteor chase? By holding us captive again?"

"Ugh!" Starlee shouts, pulling a second weapon out of her jumpsuit. Both her paws are outstretched now, one aiming at Becka, the other at me. "*I* didn't hold you captive. My moms did. And can you blame them? They're scared. The Quarantine took away the rest of our people years ago, long before I was even born. A lot's happened to them. Then *you* chase me through the desert and track me through the mines and sneak into their base camp. They're not at fault for defending themselves." Her nostrils flare. "But I came here anyway, on my own, to help! So put down your weapons!"

Becka laughs. "You first."

"I don't think so," Starlee says, narrowing her eyes, holding her weapons a little straighter. There's a flash of orange-gold as she shifts position, and I see that she's wearing the necklace that one of her moms had on earlier.

"Please," Ari says, joining the circle. He holds out his hands, no blasters, palms open. "*Everyone!* Weapons down. Let's talk. We're on the same side!"

Becka rolls her eyes so far back into her head that I'm afraid the whole ship might tip over. "I'd like her to give us one good reason why we should trust her, after the way her parents treated us."

"I'm not my parents," she says to Becka, which, I gotta admit, isn't the worst defense.

Still: "It doesn't matter," I say. "You're not one of us. We can't trust you."

Becka nods. "Not even close."

Ari backs up a foot and takes out his own two blasters—

"See?" I say. "It's unanimous."

—and points them at *Becka and me.*

"Enough!" Ari shouts.

Becka gasps. "Ari, what are you doing?"

"Put them down, Ari," I say. A terrible, unthinkable thought occurs to me. "You . . . you're not the Minister's spy, right? *Please* tell me you're not the spy." My mind races. My eyes sting with tears.

Ari shoots the ground at my feet. The floor sparks with the blast of the stun laser. "I can't believe you'd say that. I can't believe you'd even *think* it!"

"Then what are you doing?!" Becka shouts, the blasters in her hands shaking.

"I'm just being *me*," Ari says. "Having a little faith. But you two don't trust anyone. Doubting the teachers. Doubting each other. Doubting me. How are we supposed to get through this if we can't believe in people once in a while? I'm tired of it! I know we've been through a lot. But no one on this ship is out to get you—"

"What about Hunter?" Becka interrupts.

"What about him?" Ari counters. "Just because one person let us down, that doesn't mean we shouldn't ever trust anyone else. I trusted the teachers. I trust you. And I trust Starlee. She says she's here to help us. I believe her. Maybe that makes me the *weak one*. Maybe it makes me *gullible*. I don't care! *We need to believe in people*. We need to stick together." He lowers his blasters. "Or else the mission really is over."

Becka and I look at each other, still not sure what to do.

Starlee drops her blasters too. "You need to understand," she tries to explain, "that my family won't help you because of *me*. When they got caught by the Minister, they made an agreement. They gave up their ship and volunteered to work in the mines. Agreed to stop looking for the rest of our people and keep their heads down for the rest of their lives. So technically, I'm free. I don't have to work. And when I get old enough, my parents are going to insist I leave Elvid IX and go who-knows-where by myself. They gave up their freedom . . . for mine. Now they're afraid that if they violate their agreement with the Minister, she'll take away the one thing they have left."

"You," Ari whispers.

"Me." Starlee growls. "But I can't let everyone waste this chance to put things right. If we join up, I think I might know a way to find *everyone*."

My stomach lurches. I holster my blaster.

"Join up," Becka echoes. She's looking at Ari, who nods.

"Trust each other," he says. "Stick together. All of us."

Becka stands there for a few seconds, thinking. Finally she grins at Ari, holsters her blaster, and extends a friendly hand for a Starlee to shake. "Sorry about the misunderstanding," Becka says. "Welcome aboard the PSS 118."

21

We've moved to Principal Lochner's office, which Gena and Cal cleaned up after Hunter's Rebellion. We're all here around the conference table: Me, Ari, Becka. Ming, Riya, Missi. Diana, Cal, Gena. The ship's commanding officers. (Which Ari keeps trying to call the Council of Shrew. He even printed matching T-shirts.) We're gathered to listen to Starlee's story.

"When my family was still flying around the galaxy in the Poplar," she tells us, "trying to learn about the Quarantine, we found something."

"Something that reverses it?" Missi asks. The room buzzes with excitement.

"No," Starlee answers. And the room falls silent again. "A machine. Stolen from a secret Elvidian freighter en route to the galactic core. My moms disabled the ship's engines, snuck onboard, and struck mold."

Ari squints. "Don't you mean they struck *gold*?"

Starlee raises a furry eyebrow. "That's what I said, they struck *mold*."

Ari and I look at each other. A translation hiccup, probably. The first in a while.

Becka raises her hands in the air. "Starlee, what are these called?"

"Fingerbunches?" Starlee answers. "Why?"

"No reason."

"Anyway," Starlee continues, "the machine is a sensor. Calibrated to detect the precise radiation signature the Quarantine puts out when it sends people away. My moms took it back to our home solar system, which, like yours, is empty."

"Then what happened?" Riya whispers.

"It worked," Starlee says. "They got a signal. They tracked it."

My heart thumps inside my chest. The Quarantine can be hacked. It can be *followed*.

"Tracked it where?" Ari asks, practically spilling out of his chair. Becka grabs Diana's hand.

"Does your ship have the tech to display a map of the galaxy?" Starlee asks.

"Ship," I call out. "Can you—"

"*I HEARD HER. DO I HAVE THE TECH TO DISPLAY A MAP?! PLEASE. WHAT DO YOU THINK I AM, A GLORIFIED TOASTER?!*"

"I think the ship means *yes*," I say.

"*OF COURSE I HAVE THE TECH,*" the ship huffs,

insulted. *"YOU WANT STANDARD OR INFRARED? STATIC OR REAL TIME? DISTANCE IN LD? AU? LIGHT YEARS? PARSECS? GIGAPARSECS? HU—"*

"Okay, Ship," I interrupt. "Now you're showing off."

"Just, like, a regular map, Ship, okay?" Ari says.

"FINE." The lights dim, and a bright hologram of the Milky Way appears above the conference table, slowly spiraling over our heads. *"IT'S IN PARSECS, BY THE WAY."*

"Great," Starlee says, ignoring the ship's nonsense. She points behind her head. "Jack, can I use that access panel over there to plug in some coordinates?"

I look at Becka and Ari. She nods slowly. He throws out two thumbs up.

So I place my hand against the panel and grant Starlee access. "Our ship is your ship."

"Thanks," Starlee says, quickly typing. "Ship, I'm giving you a set of universal galactic coordinates. The Elvidian map you have in your databanks should be able to plot the points against public star charts." A red dot appears on the far edge of the Perseus Arm. "That's my home planet. Meerkat Prime."

"She's a meerkat?" Becka says quietly into my ear.

"So not a lion," I say.

"I was closer," Ari mumbles.

"Great, Ship," Starlee continues. "Now draw a straight line from Meerkat Prime to the very opposite end of the galaxy. One end to the other."

"*AHEM*," the ship grunts.

Starlee looks at us.

"It wants you to say please," I explain.

Starlee rolls her eyes—

"*I SAW THAT.*"

—and asks: "Ship, *please* draw a straight line through the map, from one end to the other."

"*I'D BE HAPPY TO,*" the ship chirps. A line appears on the map, cutting the galaxy in half.

"That's what happened," Starlee says, pointing up at the line. "That was the problem. The machine—this Quarantine scanner or sensor or whatever you want to call it—could only detect a *direction*. It could only tell us which way everyone went. Not where they stopped. All we had was a straight line through the galaxy."

"What did you do next?" Becka asks.

"The only thing we could. We searched. For years and years. We started at Meerkat Prime and followed the line. System by system. It was mostly empty void. No ships, hardly even any planets. We didn't find anything promising. When the Minister finally found us, we were low on fuel and food and water. My parents just . . . gave up without a fight."

We continue to stare up at the Milky Way, as the galaxy spins above our heads.

"But now," Starlee adds, leaning forward, "everything's changed. Now, we have another line to cross with the old one."

I don't get it. But Ari does. Missi too, apparently.

"Ship," they say at the same time.

Missi blushes. "You go."

Ari shakes his head. "No, you, Science Officer Tinker."

Missi looks up at the map. "Ship, can you please draw another line? Start at Earth this time and run it to the other side of the galaxy, crossing over Starlee's first line, okay? You can draw it going anywhere. It's just an example."

"*GOTCHA*." Even the ship sounds excited. And now I understand.

One line isn't enough. The galaxy is too impossibly big. But *two* lines, heading in the same direction, crossing each other in the middle . . .

Ari's eyes twinkle, reflecting the billions of stars dancing above us. "X marks the spot."

22

Becka's log! Missed me? Of course you did. And if you've been thinking to yourself: *Hey! When do I get to see how awesome it's gonna be when Becka's captain?* Well, the wait is over.

My turn.

After the Battle of SpaceMart Station, Ari didn't wanna be captain for that long, bless his sweet heart. But Jack and I would both live in that chair forever if we could. I lost the first rock-paper-scissors game fair and square, so he got next. And we set an alarm in our rings so we'd each have the exact same amount of time. As soon as Starlee was done explaining her whole "X marks the spot" thing, the alarm went off.

Jack saluted me. "Captain Pierce. What now?"

"Now," I said, all business, "we save everyone."

Ari shuddered and smiled at the same time. "Chills." He showed Gena the goosebumps on his arm. "Did you get chills? I totally got chills." Then he looked around at the rest of the room and I guess realized that he was being a little weird again. "Sorry. Proceed."

"Only one option," I said. "We get that machine. Take it back to our system. Use it to scan for the Quarantine and . . ."

"And find out where both our peoples went," Starlee finished.

"Exactly," I said. "So the sensor. Where is it?"

"That's the problem," said Starlee. "As far as my parents know, the Elvidians never found it. It's still hooked up to our ship. It's onboard the Poplar."

Riya leaned forward. "Why's that a problem?"

Jack's face went pale. "Because Starlee said that the Minister *took* the Poplar."

Starlee nodded. "Yeah. She did."

That hung in the air for a moment until Missi asked: "Took it where?"

Starlee breathed in deep. "Inside her palace."

There were a variety of reactions to that piece of news:

Me: "So how do we break in?"

Riya and Diana high-fived.

Missi activated the holographic notes app on her ring so she could take down any instructions.

The ship: *"CAN YOU LEAVE ME IN ORBIT?"*

Cal shouted: "Gena and I can stay!"

Gena: "Oh sure, that's no problem. We can definitely stay. Totally. No problem. Did I say that already?"

Ming: "Whatever you need, Captain."

Ari: "So is the Minister's palace, like, a volcano with a giant skull built into it?"

Jack: "Another impossible mission."

I glared at him. We were past the time for doubts. Hadn't we *just* finished that blaster showdown in the mess hall where Ari talked sense into us? But fine. I cracked my knuckles.

Inspirational captain speech time. I touched the nearest access panel and scrolled though the music data bank, settling on an instrumental track from the score of *Neptune Attacks: The Movie*. The perfect epic background music for the occasion.

"Impossible?" I looked around the table. "What, are you scared?"

Jack narrowed his eyes. "No."

"Liar," I said. He looked down at his hands. "Of course you're scared. We're all scared. Diana, remember when Mom took the training stabilizers off your ion propulsion scooter?"

Diana laughed. "When I was six?"

"Yeah." I could still picture Diana in the yard in front of our housing pod, crying for our parents to put the stabilizers back on. "How'd you feel?"

"Scared."

"But what did you do anyway?"

"I . . . I tried. Skinned my knee twice that first day. But I tried."

I squeezed her hand just as the music started to build.

"Riya, remember district basketball semifinals against St. Andrews in fifth grade?"

We lost that game, like we lost every game against St. Andrews. But we were neck and neck the whole time, and the final score was *so* close.

"How could I forget?" Riya said.

"And when you took that foul shot in the fourth quarter, how did you feel?"

"Scared."

"But what did you do anyway?"

"Tried."

"Missi, were you scared at Model UN last year?"

"Of course."

"Gena, Cal—were you scared when you joined the others in fighting back against Hunter? And when we put you in charge of all the other kids?"

"Yes," they both answered, speaking above the swelling soundtrack.

"Ming, were you scared when we appointed you acting captain?"

"Absolutely."

"Ari, Jack—were you scared when we sneaked out of Elvidian jail last year? When we fought our way back to Earth? When we escaped the robot war?"

"Yes."

Bring it home, Becka.

I smacked the table with both my fists, in perfect time with a crash of cymbals. "And what did we all do anyway?"

197

"We tried!"

I looked at Starlee—who smiled at me—then at every other face in the room, one by one. "Yeah, we're all scared now too. Yeah, this is gonna be tough. But we only have one choice: To try. Nothing's impossible. We've proven that over and over. So we keep going. Together."

"Aye, aye, Captain," Jack said, saluting.

Told you I'd rock at all this captain stuff.

Ari saluted too. Then the others. "Aye, aye, Captain!" they shouted, just as the music hit its peak and began to slow. I'd timed it flawlessly.

I saluted back at them. "At ease, crew. No time to lose. Ming, get the ship into orbit. Riya, I want a full inventory of supplies—weapons, fuel, everything. Jack, run a diagnostic on the light speed engine. We can't afford any surprises there. Missi, work with Starlee to collect every detail she knows about the Poplar and the Minister's palace. Ari, check the public records. Look for any information that might help us get inside the palace. Diana, I need you to prep a shuttle. See what you can do to boost shields and speed. Cal, Gena, spread the word. Call a full school assembly for, say, oh-nine-hundred hours tomorrow morning. We have a heist to plan. Dismissed."

I glanced over at Ari. "And may Sol burn brightly till the end."

Then I winked at Jack, holding up a sideways empty fist and releasing it in the air. Mic-drop motion. "Now *that's* how you captain a ship."

23

"Sigma Base to Sigma Leader. Come in, Sigma Leader."

Becka, Starlee, and I are on the ground. In disguise. Deep undercover. Ari's running comms from a nearby shuttle. And we're all a little tense.

"Wait," Becka whispers. We've got buds in our ears, connected to Ari. "Am *I* Sigma Leader?"

Ari huffs through the comms. "Who else? You're the captain now."

"What's *my* call sign, Ari?" I ask.

"You're Sigma Two. And don't use real names over this channel. That's the whole point."

"Am I Sigma One?" asks Starlee.

"Ten-four," Ari tells her.

"Is that a yes?"

"Sure is!"

"Hold on," I say. "Why am *I* Sigma Two? Why isn't Starlee Sigma Two?" I lean over toward her rhinogoat suit. "No offense."

"None taken," Starlee says.

"She's our guest," Ari explains. "And don't use real names!"

"Got it," Becka says. "So Ari—you called us. Is something wrong?"

"Nah. Just testing the comms equipment. And how many times do I have to say *don't use real names?*"

Though the comms receiver, I can't tell if Becka is laughing or groaning. Probably both.

"Fine, Sigma Base," she says. "But let's keep radio chatter to a minimum unless something's up."

"Ten-four, Sigma Leader. Sigma Base out."

Planning for this mission took three days, with everyone working around the clock. Ari and Missi gathered information. Riya, Diana, and I made sure the ship and shuttles were ready. Ming, Gena, and Cal kept everything—and everyone—running smoothly and in sync. If only Principal Lochner could see us now.

I've gotta hand it to her: Becka makes a decent captain.

Even if the whole "wearing full-body disguises to blend in" plan is getting a little old.

"And here," the Elvidian tour guide is saying, "you can see the absolutely perfect brushstrokes. They really struck mold here with this gallery. Of course, *any* painting of the Minister is perfect."

Murmurs of agreement from around the room.

"Still," the tour guide continues, "sometimes, a re-creation of the Minister's likeness is so magnificent as to be extra perfect."

More nods. Another rhinogoat—a real one, not a human in disguise—wipes a tear.

The thing they don't tell you about climbing inside full-body rhinogoat costumes—designed and fabricated by Missi, Ari, and a small army of Pencils—is how freakin' hot it is in here. Next time we mock up giant alien suits and spend all day walking around inside them, I'm splurging for some AC.

"This way, please," the Elvidian says. "Next, we will visit the Hall of Statues."

The plan is simple. We didn't have to break into the Minister's giant, gold-plated palace. (Not a skull volcano, which Ari found "disappointing.") Because you can just take an official tour of "the most magnificent structure in the galaxy." The Minister thinks so highly of herself, she let us walk right in.

Which is why Becka, Starlee, and I are roaming around in here, dressed as rhinogoats, hiding in plain sight. Ari's running point in the getaway shuttle, which is parked in one of the public lots. And everyone else is onboard the 118, in orbit, just inside the range of the light speed jamming. Far enough away that they can make a quick getaway without us if things go south. Close enough that if they have to come get us, they don't have to go through Orientation again.

"Sigma Base to Sigma Leader. Come in, Sigma Leader."

"Yes, Sigma Base?" Becka says.

"Can you step a little closer to that painting at your three o'clock?"

The rhinogoat masks are equipped with cameras that feed into the shuttle screens. Ari sees what we see.

"Approaching now," Becka says. Starlee and I join her. "What is it? A clue? Are we in danger?"

Ari breathes into his mic. "What? No! It's just a cool painting. See how the Minister's eyes are all sparkly? And she's totally bald in this one! I like that look. Very villain chic."

Becka backs up again. "Minimal. Radio. Chatter."

"Oops," Ari says. "Right. Sorry. Sigma Base out. For real this time."

We follow the tour guide from the Gallery (of pictures of the Minister) to the Hall of Statues (of statues of the Minister) to the Portico of Speeches (where you can play holographic video clips of the Minister's greatest hits). It's all pretty on-brand.

"Dear citizens . . ." a giant holographic Minister head is saying.

"Is this her speech from the last trisolar festival?" some Elvidian tourist asks us.

I panic. But Becka's on it.

"Love that one," she grunts from inside her rhinogoat suit.

The Elvidian nods. "So inspiring."

". . . which is why," the Minister recording is saying, "I will be requisitioning additional mandatory labor. These patriots will be tasked with the great duty of polishing all official statues and monuments that have been built in my honor . . ."

"Yeah," Becka grunts. "So inspiring." She steps away from the alien and speaks into her mic. "Sigma Base? We've entered the Portico of Speeches. The main palace corridor is visible, as expected. Commencing Shrew drop now."

"Please be gentle with him," Ari says over comms.

"Of course," I promise, removing Doctor Shrew from my pocket. Next to me, Starlee activates the Pencil we lent her, and the mech suit materializes on the ground. I place Doctor Shrew gently inside and latch him in.

"I still don't understand," Starlee says as Doctor Shrew trots off, with Ari remote-controlling the suit from the shuttle. "Couldn't you have automated the mech? Why bother putting your pet in there?"

The mech—which looks and moves a little bit like the bottom half of a very tiny *T. rex*—shuffles to the other side of the room. *See-zee. See-zee.* The nearby Elvidian tourist looks down . . . and screams.

"Beast!" The Elvidian runs down the hallway. "Keep back!"

Other aliens—rhinogoats, Statues of Liberty, babymen—don't seem to mind. But any Elvidians in Doctor

Shrew's path scatter like bowling pins whenever he comes near.

"That's why," Becka says. "Of all the things in the universe, they're afraid of hamsters."

Doctor Shrew—*see-zee, see-zee, see-zee*—scurries out of sight.

"Good luck, Doctor," Ari whispers.

Finally, the tour ends and we see our destination: an enormous gift shop filled with Minister souvenirs. Multiple cashiers in each corner of the room. A small café in the center, serving cones of half-alive meat. A little crab claw reaches up out of one cone and scratches itself on what's either its nose or its eye or both. A Statue of Liberty alien plucks one up from its holder, shouts "Yum!" and eats the whole thing in one bite.

I feel a little sick and look away. Past the café. To the outer walls . . .

"There," Starlee points. "The Poplar."

One of a dozen glass-encased ships displayed in a circle around the edges of the room. Trophies.

"Yes!" I whisper-cheer, punching the air with a giant rhinogoat fist.

It's right where we expected to find it, thanks to the images of the gift shop posted all over ElvNet, "The Galaxy's Premier Social Media Network."

The Poplar is smaller than I imagined. About the width of one of our shuttles, and maybe three or four times the length. It's also by far the ugliest ship I have ever seen, and we flew the PSS 118 before the upgrades. The Poplar is greenish-gray and lumpy, built in bulby segments, like a caterpillar cut in half and left to rot. But it's here. It's really here.

I'm hugely relieved . . . for about a millisecond.

"Ari?" Becka says, staring in the opposite direction. "Are you seeing this?"

"Yeah," Ari responds.

Becka is facing a wall at the far end of the gift shop, past the café and the circle of ships. There's a screen in front of her, displaying about twenty faces in a row. Mostly alien. A couple of robots. And—

"Is that us?" I say.

I hear Ari gulp through the comms. It's us. Me, Ari, and Becka, underneath the caption:

Public Enemies. Armed & Dangerous. Wanted Dead or Alive.

Becka shudders and turns back toward the Poplar. "Ignore it. We're still disguised. This changes nothing. Let's get this over with. Ready, Sigma Base?"

Around the room, other tourists are taking in the ships, sitting down to eat, or browsing the shelves.

"Aye, aye. I'm all set. Doctor Shrew is already on his way back to the shuttle. Commencing Phase Two on your mark."

"Everyone in position," Becka orders.

There's only one way out of the gift shop: back through the gold-plated corridor that leads to the Portico of Specches. I step toward the corridor, thumb ready to click my Pencil. Becka and Starlee walk in the opposite direction, toward the glass case surrounding the Poplar.

"Do it," Becka orders.

"Phase Two commencing," Ari says, before shrieking through the first mini-speaker dropped by Doctor Shrew. That was his mission: to distribute small comms devices throughout the public spaces in the palace. Easier for him to do than us, given his size and the fact that Elvidians don't like going near him. And harder for the job to be traced back.

"Oh my goodness!" Ari calls out from a speaker. Even from the other end of the corridor, it's loud enough to hear. "It's the Minister! In person! Oh, hello, Minister! I just *love* you! Can I get your autograph? *Yes!* Oh, thank you!"

The possibility of meeting the Minister is all it takes. Everyone stampedes out of the room, meat cones thrown to the ground. (They crawl out of sight.) Even the tour guide bolts. The cashiers too. And as soon as the last of them have gone, I take up position.

"Scanning the entrance now," Ari says, examining my helmet's camera feed. "Calculating dimensions. Generating code. Transmitting to your Pencil and . . . done. Go for it, Sigma Two. You're locked and loaded."

I click my Pencil and release the nanobots. They materialize in the hallway beyond, just outside the gift ship. A door. Ari's built a door to fit in this exact spot to hide us from anyone passing by. It won't hold if someone charges in. But it's something.

"I even added a little one-way porthole," Ari explains. "See?"

I peek through the small circle of glass that Ari programmed into the metallic door.

"You can see out," he says. "But the other side is a mirror."

"Nice job," Becka says, removing her rhinogoat helmet. Starlee and I do the same. We're all sweaty, hair matted down to our heads.

"Oh!" Ari yells through another speaker. "You're *here* now! Hello, Minister! I just love all your . . . ministering! I can't imagine anyone being more ministery than you!" He squeals with delight. "And hugs all around? How lovely! Of *course* I'd be up for brunch with you one of these days."

His voice is farther down the corridor now, as is the sound of the crowd jogging toward it. The hope is that Ari can lead them in circles long enough for us to get what we came for.

Becka and Starlee, gripping blowtorches, exchange nods. This is the big unknown. The one thing that Ari and Missi couldn't confirm in their research: How protected is the Poplar? Is the glass breakable? Alarmed? Even if Becka and Starlee manage to cut through, will guards storm in before we can grab the sensor and get out?

Becka and Starlee start cutting away and—nothing. No alarm. No guards. Just another announcement from Ari, shouting through a third speaker.

"Why, Minister! Have you been working out? You have to tell me your secret! Can I feel your muscles?"

In seconds, Becka and Starlee are inside the display case. Seconds after that, a hatch on the Poplar opens in response to Starlee's touch.

"Keep watch," Becka says to me.

I salute and stare out through the one-way mirror in Ari's door.

It's kind of creepy, looking through a window that doesn't show me on the other side. An Elvidian family walks down the corridor, only inches away. A tall Statue of Liberty follows, chatting with one of those "baby" aliens. He's floating at eye level in this hover-booster seat. And here comes a line of Elvidian soldiers wearing their coin-covered metal armor.

I peer into the hallway for one minute. Two. Five.

"What's taking so long?" I ask Becka and Starlee.

"We're working on it!" Becka shouts back.

I look around at the rest of the gift shop. Minister shirts. Minister hats. Minister bobbleheads. I flip over a snow globe that looks like the surface of Elvid IV, the Minister's other favorite planet. Where they kept us prisoner over the summer. Miniature towers of black glass rise up from the bottom of the crystal ball. And when I turn the snow globe right-side up again, bright purple electricity falls from the top, raining down on the towers and melting them into dust—before they rise up again, resetting.

"Weird," Ari says, startling me. I'd forgotten that he can see what I see.

"No kidding," I say back, pulling a Minister doll off the shelf instead. I pull the cord at its back: "Long live the Minister! Long live the Minister! Long live the Minister!"

On second thought, no more browsing.

I look back through the window: More rhinogoats walk by. A zebradactyl. Two Elvidian soldiers, marching with purpose down the hallway, weapons pointed at a third alien between them . . . My heart skips a beat. Long dark cloak. Hood pulled back. Lines wrinkling a face that's seen everything.

"Bale Kontra," I whisper.

"What?" Ari says over comms, except I also hear his voice through a speaker somewhere nearby. "Sorry," he says, asking again, only in my ears: "What's he doing here?"

"He must be their prisoner," I tell him, feeling an overwhelming surge of guilt. It's the only explanation. "When we named him in the library, it must have . . . We have to help him."

"How?" Ari asks at the exact same time Becka says, "Absolutely not."

She steps out of the Poplar. "We found the sensor.

Starlee's still trying to get it unhooked. We don't have time to get distracted. You saw those posters. *They're looking for us.* We need to get off this planet ASAP."

"It's my fault he got captured," I say.

"You don't know that," Becka argues.

"I fed the information to the library, and now Elvidian soldiers are pointing guns at him. You think that's a coincidence?"

"You had to," Becka says. "It was the only way to find the Poplar."

"Doesn't make it right," I say. "He helped us. He tried to help my dad too. And I sold him out."

The guards and their prisoner disappear around a corner.

"We have a mission," Becka reminds me. "I need you here. *I'm* the captain now and that's an order."

Before Becka can object again, I remove the Pencil-made door, step through, and put it back. I turn around to face her through the window. Even though I can't see her anymore, I know she's still there.

"I have to do this," I say. *Do I?* Am I actually making the right call? But there's no time to think. Bale Kontra is already out of sight. I have to move. "Get the scanner. Get out of the palace. If I don't meet you back at the shuttle in . . ." With my ring, I project the time in my palm and set an alarm. ". . . one hour, leave without me."

"No," Ari whispers in my ear. I can hear the fear in his voice. "What happened to sticking together?"

"I'm sorry," I say. "Complete the mission. Get back to our system and find our people."

"Don't do this, Jack," Becka says. I hear her in my ear and through the doorway. "I'm not asking as the captain anymore. I'm asking as your friend. *Please.*"

But I switch off my comms unit, shut down the camera feed, and turn to follow Bale Kontra deeper into the palace.

24

Bale Kontra's guards lead him through a door that clicks open only after a retinal scan. Luckily, the door takes a few seconds to close behind them, and I manage to wedge my giant rhinogoat foot inside before it seals up again. We're now in an out-of-the-way section of the palace, off limits to the public.

These hallways are dark and quiet. No gold. Just plain black crystal walls that remind me of Elvid IV. Eventually, the soldiers arrive at another door and shove Bale Kontra inside. He doesn't resist. The door closes behind him. And, weapons held tight, the soldiers take up their posts on either side.

Here goes nothing.

Becka's not the only one who can try the same trick twice.

I'm still around the corner out of sight. I take out my Pencil, write the words *Decoy Jack* in the air, and click. I write another set of code to print my jetpack, which

I strap to the decoy's back and sync to my ring. Finally I shove him out into the corridor, in full view of the guards.

They immediately raise their weapons.

"Who are you?!"

"This is a restricted zone!"

"Is that—?

"Facial recognition scanning now."

"It is! The Minister personally put out a security alert for this one."

"Put your hands behind your head!"

"Jacksonville Graham, Umjerrylochner Enemy Number One! Stop right there!"

"On your knees!"

"What's that on your back?!"

"Take it off!"

I remote-activate the jetpack, and the closed corridor immediately fills with smoke. The crystal walls shake with the explosion of sound. I angle the jetpack upward, tug on one of the clutches to turn Decoy Jack around, and send him barreling in the opposite direction—down the hall, away from the soldiers.

It's hard to control. The jetpack shoots Decoy Jack through a wall, leaving a crater in the stone. Coughing into their comms devices, the soldiers take off after him.

Leaving me completely alone.

I don't have much time.

I sprint to the door. Locked. An alien voice shouts directly into my brain. "**ENTRY BY AUTHORIZATION ONLY. PASSCODE REQUIRED.**"

"Oh, come on!" I scream, banging on the door.

"**PASSCODE REJECTED.**"

Think, Jack. Think!

"**PASSCODE REJECTED.**"

"Ah! Stop saying that!"

"**PASSCODE REJECTED.**"

What would they use as a passcode? It could be anything. Numbers. Letters. Alien words I've never even heard of . . .

"Long live the Minister?"

The door clicks open. "**PASSCODE ACCEPTED.**"

I like Ari's catchphrase better.

The prison cell is dark. I can barely see Bale Kontra. He's sitting alone, hands chained by what look like tubes of lava. His hood is pulled back and he's staring at me, open mouthed.

"What is going on?!" he demands.

"Um, Bale Kontra, sir?" I pull off my rhinogoat helmet. "It's me. I'm here to rescue you."

He looks up, eyes wide.

"Jack?!" he whisper-shouts, trying to shoot up out of his chair, but the lava chains somehow pull him back down. He grunts, and I can tell he's in pain. "What are you doing here? Get out of this place. Run!"

"I came to help. It's my fault that you were caught.

We were trying to find out about the Quarantine, so we went to the library on Wyzardia—"

"Jack," Bale Kontra tries. But I keep going, a light year a minute.

"We gave them all the knowledge we had, but it wasn't enough. So I told my biggest secret. I should've thought more clearly about the consequences. I mean, I knew we were putting you at risk. But I hoped the information wouldn't find its way to the Minister. That you'd be okay."

"Jack," he tries again.

"And I'm so sorry. You did everything you could to help us. And in exchange, I . . . I . . ."

Am I *crying*? I can't help it. This feels like the last straw. Like my family's Jenga tower of mistakes is finally coming crashing down at the sight of this almost-stranger who tried to help us. This person I betrayed.

"Jack!" he snaps. "Listen to me. You're wrong. You owed me nothing. I owed *you*."

I guess he's thinking of how he failed to stop my dad from triggering the Quarantine.

"But the past doesn't matter now," he goes on. "What matters is that this is not your fault. The Minister has suspected me of treachery for nearly a full cycle. You may have provided the confirmation, but she would have learned my true loyalties soon enough. I've been hard at work. Disseminating long-secret information. Laying the groundwork for dissent. Quietly stoking resistance against her and her allies."

"All the more reason for me to get you out of here," I say. "We have a shuttle. We can—"

"I can't go with you," he says. "These chains. They can only be unlocked by the key that bound them to me in the first place. Any tampering will detonate the explosive device hidden inside."

"There has to be a way—"

"There *isn't*. Not for you. But I am not as powerless as I seem. I have my own allies."

I hear shouting in the corridor. Still far away, but moving closer.

"Isn't there anything I can do?" I ask desperately.

He narrows his eyes. "It may not be safe."

"I don't care."

Bale Kontra nods. "When you get into orbit, transmit this exact phrase on a wide-beam frequency."

"Long live the Minister?" I joke.

He laughs. I made an alien laugh, which has to count for something. "The phrase is: *When the night grows dark, the stars shine brightest.* Repeat it for me."

"When the night grows dark," I say, "the stars shine brightest."

"Excellent. Now go. Get off this planet before it's too late. Find your people. Make things right."

"We will," I say, placing the helmet back on my head. "We will."

25

"I'm almost back," I say into my comms unit, speed-walking toward the spot where we parked the shuttle. "Where *are* you guys? Delta Base? Gamma Base? I forget the call sign, Ari! But who cares? Come in, Ari! Please respond."

Nothing.

I break into a run and try the 118. "Ming, come in. Ship, do you read me? *Is anyone out there?!*"

Again, nothing. Until—*screech*—my earpiece shrieks out a horrible, high-pitched noise. We're being jammed. Not good. It's so loud in my ears that I have to pull off my rhinogoat helmet and—

"Hello, Jack," the Minister says. In person. She's standing across the concrete platform, which has been cleared of ships—including our shuttle. A cluster of Elvidian soldiers surrounds the Minister, who's standing over Becka, Ari, and Starlee. They're kneeling on the ground. Costumes off, hands tied, mouths gagged.

I drop my helmet to the ground. I doubt I'll need it anymore. "What do you want?" I yell to her, channeling as much Becka-style confidence as I can muster. But I'm literally shaking in my boots.

Escape Plan A is toast. I look at Starlee, trying to see if she's going to be able to carry out Plan B. Her eyes are wide. Her whole body is shaking. I can't tell.

The Minister laughs. So I guess that's two aliens I made laugh today.

This one's not as fun.

"I *want* what I've *always* wanted, Jack," the Minister says, walking toward me, her black cloak flowing to the floor. The top of her scepter crackles like a ball of barely contained lightning. She emphasizes every third or fourth word by slamming the scepter on the ground. With each bang, the lightning flashes purple and black, and the concrete platform cracks into spider webs beneath the staff.

"To keep this galaxy *safe*." *Bang.*

"To keep it *stable*." *Bang.*

"And most of all, to *stop* being *interfered* with by *aliens* who do not *understand* what they are *playing* with." *Bang. Bang. Bang. Bang. Bang.*

"Funny," I say, stalling for time, wracking my brain for a way out of this. "I'd say we want pretty much the same thing."

She's still walking toward me. "I don't have time for this. Whatever you think you were doing in my palace—it's over. Even now, we are scanning every inch of space around this glorious planet for your associates. Your friends on that infernal ship will not survive."

I glance at Starlee again. She shimmies and twists against the ropes binding her arms. I'm guessing that means she can't reach our backup plan: her mom's necklace with the whistle, which Starlee swiped from her before coming after us. The Poplar's proximity remote starter.

"Except you missed something," I say to the Minister.

The Minister slams her scepter down on the platform. The stone floor cracks outward in three directions, like a moonquake with her at the epicenter. "I don't *miss* things," she says.

"Sure you do. Should we count them? One. You missed something when we escaped from Elvid IV a few months ago. Two. You missed something when we refueled our ship without you noticing. Three. You missed something when you tried to turn our system's robots against us—but half of them fought back and helped us anyway. Do you want me to keep going?"

She shrugs. "Minor setbacks. All due to a single weakness in my field of vision that has now been dealt with. Thanks to you, the betrayer Bale Kontra—"

"Yeah, yeah," I interrupt. "Bale Kontra's been captured. I know. What *you* don't know is that he wasn't our only contact on your side. We had another spy."

She keeps walking forward—but I see it. The slight hesitation in her step. The worry.

"If you knew of another turncoat in my administration, you would have traded that information for knowledge on Wyzardia, my favorite honeypot."

I shrug. "Would I? Giving the library Bale Kontra's name got us what we came for. Why would I reveal my *other* secret?"

The Minister points backward with her scepter. "What you came for? You mean this child and her hopeless family?"

"Yup," I say brightly. "And if you don't release my friends right now, I'll never tell you who the other traitor is."

The Minister—only feet away now—circles me. "Ah, Jack. The sentimentality exhibited by your species is . . . quaint. But fine." She flicks her wrist. "I agree to your terms. I will release your two compatriots—"

"And Starlee," I say.

"Yes, fine, *and* the other child. Your information for your friends." She lifts her scepter slightly in the air. "Release them."

Three of her Elvidian soldiers untie my friends' hands and lower their gags. Becka stands and cracks her neck; Ari does a wide stretch, like he's just woken up from a long nap; and Starlee shakes her mane, waving her hair left and right.

Why isn't she taking it out?! Her hands are free! What is she waiting for?!

The Minister stops circling me and glares into my

eyes. "I've fulfilled my end of the bargain. Your turn."

"Do it!" I yell at Starlee. "Do it now!"

But Starlee just looks down at the floor as the Minister cackles. "Looking for this?"

She holds up the necklace in her pale, claw-like fingers. The orange-golden whistle sparkles in the sunlight.

"I'm sorry," Starlee says.

"Please," the Minister continues. "You think I didn't know that you clumsily accessed that old ship? You didn't stop for a moment to wonder why I would display some of my enemies' most prized possessions for all to see? Out in the open? Insufficiently guarded?"

See-zee.

A faint sound from somewhere beyond the platform. The Minister doesn't seem to hear it.

"I do so love setting a good trap," she says. "When will you learn that your small brains are no match for me?"

See-zee. Louder. Coming closer.

The Minister still doesn't notice. "Guards, take them away."

See-zee.

In a slow-motion blur of silver and brown and beige, Doctor Shrew—still inside his mech suit—leaps in the air. Five, ten, twenty feet high.

"No way," I whisper.

The soldiers all see him. They shrink away in disgust, clearing even more room around the startled Minister.

Doctor Shrew is up and over the platform, descending fast. The Minister raises a hand to block her face. The hand holding the whistle. Which Doctor Shrew grabs with his tiny teeth and pries from between the Minister's fingers, before hopping away and landing at Ari's feet.

"Good boy!" Ari picks up Doctor Shrew and scratches behind his ears, plucking the whistle from his mouth. "He must've thought this was a carrot."

Ari passes the whistle to Starlee, who immediately blows five notes.

The ground starts rumbling: a different sort of moonquake.

"*I said, take them away!*" the Minister shouts at her guards.

But it's too late.

"Get down!" Starlee yells, and we hit the deck. A nearby wall of the palace explodes outward in a shower of glass and gold and concrete. From the ground, with my hands covering the top of my head, I hear the ship before I see it. It makes an almost-alive shrieking sound as it barrels onto the tarmac.

There's shooting all around me.

The Minister is screaming at her guards. "Get them!"

My ears are ringing. I stand and stumble away from the Minister's voice, dodging laser bolts crisscrossing the platform.

"In here!" Starlee shouts, as the door to her ship falls open.

We sprint inside. The hatch closes. The noise from the platform instantly disappears.

Starlee freezes in the small corridor, her breathing heavy. Tears pool in her eyes. But the ship rocks from laser fire, and Ari puts a hand on her shoulder. "We've gotta go," he says.

Starlee nods, blinking back tears. She leads us toward the Poplar's cockpit. The ship rocks again and Starlee slams her hand against a big blue button on the low ceiling.

"Shields," she explains, placing a hand on the pilot's chair, tracing the seatback with her fingers. But after a moment she says, "I don't think I can fly." She holds up her shaky paws. "I'm too unsteady. Now that the Minister's found us . . ."

"You're worried about your family," Ari sums up.

She nods. "They're in danger."

Ari gives her shoulder a sympathetic pat. "We know what that's like."

"Can *you* fly this thing?" I ask him.

He leaps into the pilot's seat. Becka sits next to him as copilot, me behind him, and Starlee to my right. "Only one way to find out."

"Aren't you all terrified?" Starlee asks.

Ari flips a switch dramatically and goes, "Not my first rodeo." He immediately cracks up at himself. "I've always wanted to say that. I don't even know what a rodeo is."

Becka turns back to Starlee. "Of course we're terrified. We're always terrified, remember? But we try anyway. We keep going. Together."

Starlee nods and buckles up, which reminds the rest of us to do the same.

"Ari," Becka says calmly. Through the front window of the Poplar, we're still being fired on. But the shields are holding. And it's so quiet inside the ship that you could hear a pin drop. "Let's go home."

26

The moment we pull away from the surface, a squadron of triangular Elvidian fighters comes out of nowhere and chases us into orbit. One purple lightning bolt after another strikes the Poplar's shields. Thankfully, Ari aced the midterm on evasive maneuvers: barrel rolls, breaks and drops, pitchbacks. But it's not enough. We're outgunned.

"Ming," I say into the Poplar's comms device, hoping they can hear me. "Take the 118 and get out of here. We'll catch up."

"Starlee!" Becka yells. "How's that light speed engine coming?!"

"I'm trying!" Starlee yells back to Becka. The ship is hit again and Ari throws us into a defensive spiral.

I click the comms into wide beam.

"What are you doing?" Becka shouts.

"I need to transmit something. Bale Kontra asked."

"What, *now?*"

"Yes, now." I grab the mic and speak into it. "When the night is dark, the stars shine brightest. Okay? *When the night is dark, the stars shine brightest!*"

I half-expect this to trigger some instant reaction. For the ships to stop chasing us. For Bale Kontra's allies to come to our rescue. For *something* to happen. But nothing does. Except we take more fire against the rear shields.

"That was such a good catchphrase!" Ari shouts, his adrenaline obviously through the roof. "Wish I'd thought of it!" He slams down on the starboard thrusters and kicks us into another spin.

"Shields at half-strength!" Becka tells us. "Any day now!"

"Got it!" Starlee finally shouts, engaging the Poplar's light speed engine and sending us hurtling through space, toward home.

"I knew it was here somewhere," Starlee says when we reemerge in our own solar system. We all exhale.

The plan hasn't changed: Use the scanner to figure out which way the Quarantine took the other humans. Cross-reference the trajectory with the data from Starlee's system. X marks the spot. But first—

"Whoa," Ari whispers.

—we had to come back here.

SpaceMart Station, where we left Principal Lochner and the teachers. Where we left the robots fighting each other for control of the system. Instead of the chaos of battle, everything's quiet now. The station looks intact, at least from this distance. But it's still sitting inside a bubble of light speed jamming, so we couldn't bring the Poplar in too close right away. Instead, we're on approach the old fashioned way, with regular engines.

"Who won the battle?" Ari wonders out loud.

There's debris everywhere. Dozens—maybe hundreds—of destroyed ships. As we get closer, I can see that part of the station *is* missing. The damage has been welded over with a patchwork of plates. Maybe to keep the oxygen in, even though robots don't breathe.

A good sign.

"PSS 118," Becka tries on a broadcast channel, as Ari brings us in closer to the station. "Come in, 118. Ming? Missi? Riya? Diana? You out there?"

Nothing. We don't see the ship on our scopes, and no return transmission comes through.

"What do we do if they're not here?" Ari asks.

"We finish the mission ourselves," Becka says firmly. She turns to Starlee. "You already have the data from your own system, right? That gives us half of the equation?"

Starlee nods. "Yes."

"How long do you need before the scanner can tell us which way the humans went?"

Starlee pulls on a lever and spins a small wheel. "One of your hours," she says. "Give or take."

An hour. I can't decide if that's too long or not long enough, given the magnitude of what we're hoping to learn.

"Start it," Becka orders. "The sooner we get that data, the sooner we can leave."

Starlee nods. "I'm on it. Scanner set."

". . . in, Ms. Pierce. This is the 118. Come in, Becka."

The Poplar's primary comms system is holographic, with the 3D display projected over my console. A five-inch tall ghost of Principal Lochner appears. His jacket's off. His shirt is untucked. But he's okay. He's alive.

"Principal Lochner!" I say, letting out a sigh of relief.

"I guess our side won," says Ari, beaming.

"Ah, Jack, Ari, you're here too. Good. Yes, Ari, the station is secure, and all remaining robots who were working with the Minister have been switched offline. As for you—"

"We have a scanner," Becka start to explain, but Principal Lochner cuts her off.

"I know," he says. "Ming explained everything. You've done extraordinary work. Again. We're on the 118, on the far side of the station. Bring your ship in here. We've got an airlock prepped on the station, in case the 118's hangar is too small."

"Got it," Becka says.

"What about me?" Starlee asks sheepishly.

I turn to her. "You're coming with us. We'll finish this together and find our people. *All* our people."

The ship shrieks out an alarm. Ari's hands jolt and the ship does an accidental loop-the-loop.

"What was that?" Becka asks. "Is the ship okay?"

Ari shrugs, pulling up on the flight controls, steadying us out. "I think so?"

"The ship is fine," Starlee answers. "For now."

Becka tilts around, trying to see what Starlee sees on her screen. "What do you mean, for—"

"Ah!" the Minister's voice bursts through our comms. The hologram of Principal Lochner fizzles and disappears, replaced by a projection of the Elvidian leader. "How predictable."

"She's here," Starlee says, as if we needed the announcement. "They're all here."

Becka growls. "Brake," she tells Ari. "Turn us around. I want to see."

We haven't reached the station yet. But we are inside the cone of its light speed jamming. Which is probably the only reason the army of Elvidian ships in the distance isn't already breathing down our necks.

The holographic feed flickers again, and the Minister is replaced by Principal Lochner. "What do you want?" he says, trying to sound tough. "This is Principal Jerry Lochner of the PSS 118."

The Minister returns. "I have no idea who you are and I don't care."

The hologram flickers for a moment, but the principal doesn't return.

"She's jamming comms again," Ari explains.

"Dude," Becka says to the all-powerful alien queen with the giant terrifying space army, "you're the worst. You know that?"

"Beckenham Pierce," the Minister says. "Sister: Indianapolis. Parents: Bradford and Tamworth." The color runs out of Becka's face. "Two-bedroom housing pod in Bloc 14 of the Ganymede Residential Complex. There's a stuffed tiger on the bookshelf in your room. You once pretended to break your leg so your mother would take you into Busiris and you could get a glimpse of your favorite band, which had come to play a show."

"She's trying to get in your head," I say.

"Shall I get in yours, Jack?"

I roll my eyes. "I'm Jacksonville Graham. Parents: Allentown and Nicolet. I once found a Band-Aid cooked into a mushroom calzone, but the pizza place wouldn't give me a refund."

"Oh my gosh," Ari says. "I remember that. So gross."

The Minister leans forward, her hologram closing the gap between me and the Poplar's viewscreen. "I want you to know, Jack, that I took your recommendation seriously."

"What recommendation?"

"When you alerted me to another betrayer in my midst."

When I lied to her, she means. On the platform. To convince her to free Starlee's hands.

"I gave it thought. And, granted, you were likely attempting to deceive me. But we can't be too careful, can we? It's possible that another of my advisors did betray me. So I . . . disposed of them."

"Disposed of them?" My heart suddenly crashes against my chest like a thousand bolts of lightning. My mind races with the possibilities, each worse than the next.

She smiles. "All of them."

My vision goes blurry. My hands grip the sides of my chair. The walls of the Poplar seem like they're closing in. I know that the Minister's advisers probably weren't the nicest of alien overlords. But that doesn't mean I wanted them to . . . to . . .

Becka puts a hand on mine. "You didn't do anything wrong. *She* did." Becka glares back at the hologram. "So what now? You want us to surrender?"

"Jack," Starlee whispers. "Your ship, the 118. It's broken away from the station with a bunch of other uncrewed craft. They're heading for us."

I can barely hear her. I can't stop thinking about those advisors. My fault. My fault. My fault.

"Surrender?" she repeats. "No. We're long past surrender."

"Then what do you want?!" Becka shouts.

"Only to look you three in the eye one last time before I'm finally rid of you." She holds up her scepter and, through the window, the Elvidian ships—big and small—begin racing toward us. "Goodbye."

An alarm chimes on my and Becka's rings. The captain alarm. We look to Ari, who's up next. But he clenches his eyes shut and shakes his head. "Uh-uh. No way. I can't. I'm sorry."

So Becka turns to me, her expression grim. "What now, Captain?"

27

Becka grabs me by the collar of my shirt, yanking it tight. "Get it together, Graham," she says.

Ari gently pushes her arm down, but nods in agreement. "We need you."

I blink. My fault.

"It's *not* your fault," Ari says, as if reading my mind.

"And either way," Becka adds, "there's nothing we can do to change the past. But we can keep going. We *need* to keep going."

"One step at a time," Ari says.

I look up at him. Maybe he's seen me play my mom's message. Or maybe that's just the kind of guy he is.

I breathe. One. Two. Three. "Ari? Fly us toward the 118 and its formation." A hundred robot ships are rushing toward us from the station, ready to back us up.

An Elvidian fleet, ten times the size of our ragtag forces, speeds at us from the other direction.

"Jack," Principal Lochner says through the speaker

above my head. There's no hologram, but he's found a way to transmit audio through the comms jamming. "As soon as you've formed up alongside the 118, we'll make a break for the other side of the station—toward the edge of the light speed jamming bubble. We'll get out of here. Find somewhere safe to regroup"

"Can the robots come with us?" I ask.

"No," Principal Lochner answers. "None of their ships have light speed engines."

Meaning: even if we manage to escape, we'll be on our own. And we'll be abandoning the robots who've risked so much to help us.

"The Elvidians will be in range in three minutes, Jack," Becka tells me.

"How long until we're alongside the 118?"

She grimaces. "About the same."

I nod. It's gonna be close. It's always close. I look over at Starlee, who's staring at the scanner, willing it to go faster. This time, close may not be good enough.

"You'll make it," Principal Lochner assures us. "Then we'll figure out the next step."

The next step. Slow and steady. My mom's advice is good. It got me this far. But not every moment is right for being careful. Some moments are right for my dad's instincts. For taking big chances. For having faith. For trying to change everything by making a single choice.

This is one of those times.

"No," I say back to Principal Lochner. "We can't leave."

Ari: "What?!"

Becka: "Good call."

Principal Lochner: "What do you mean?" Fear and frustration in his voice.

I try to explain. "We've started the scanner onboard the Poplar. The one that will tell us where the Quarantine leads. If we leave now, we'll have to restart the scan. It takes an hour and it's not even halfway done."

"Fine!" Principal Lochner shouts. "So we start over! We go to Ganymede or Earth or Luna. Somewhere the Quarantine also hit. Somewhere that isn't *here*."

I shake my head again. "No. The Minister and the Elvidians will follow us. This, right here, is as protected as we're ever going to be. We have a hundred ships with us, right? We'll lose that support if we run. And we'll lose the minutes that have already ticked down on the scanner. If we wait, we may never get another shot at this."

"Jack—"

"No, Principal Lochner. You need to go. Take the 118. You've got the whole school to protect. I understand. Send us the rendezvous coordinates, and we'll join you when we can. But we have to see this through."

I look at Becka and Ari and Starlee. "Right?"

I'm the captain. But this is a choice we have to make together.

Starlee nods.

With tears in his eyes, Ari says, "Right."

And with an unhesitating salute, Becka gives the loudest "Aye, aye, Captain!" of her life. She looks down and back up. "One more minute until both fleets are within range."

"Go," I tell Principal Lochner. "We'll join you when we can."

Silence on the line, until: "You're right," Principal Lochner says.

"*HE IS?*" I hear the ship ask in the background.

"Yes," agrees Stingy—er, Vice Admiral Stingy—from one of the robots' ships. "This is our last stand, whether you leave or not. It'd be an honor to have you with us."

"Sometimes," Principal Lochner says, "this old man needs to be told what's what. You're right—this is our best play. So we stay. We fight. And the minute that scanner has done its job, we make our escape. Meet up at the rendezvous coordinates I'm transmitting now."

"Ten seconds!" Becka shouts.

Nine. Eight. Seven.

Another countdown to the end.

28

We unleash everything we've got.

The 118, the Poplar, and the robot support ships have all moved closer to the station. It's big enough to give us cover, reducing the need to keep an eye on every point on the compass.

Ari spins us in a corkscrew maneuver to shake an Elvidian fighter loose, while the 118 blasts it with close-range laser cannons. Ari lifts the Poplar up and over the station and then across, down, and underneath it again, coming back out where we started—only to face another five Elvidian fighters head-on. Becka, monitoring the scanners, warns Ari about the approaching threats. Starlee shouts, "Portside shields nearing fifty percent!" And I try to shoot the Elvidians down with the Poplar's clumsy front-mounted turret, but I miss.

Comms chatter rises:

Principal Lochner: "Ship! Prep the rail gun! Redirect thirty percent rear shield power to the nose!"

Stingy: "Silicon Squadron, watch your flank. We've got incoming."

Chucklebot Seven: "We're too far! We're too—"

Principal Lochner: "Protect the Poplar!"

Creaky: "There's too many of them!"

Static. Explosions. Laser fire. Ships lost on both sides. Mostly ours.

The 118 pulls back and reorients, trying to aim its top-mounted rail gun at the fighters trailing us. Ari gets the hint and takes up position directly in front of the 118, luring the Elvidian fighters into the 118's sights. Then he brakes hard and nose-dives us under the 118. We're thrown back into our seats as the rail gun fires off a dozen rounds.

The 118 gets most of the Elvidian fighters. The remaining two fire off simultaneous shots of purple lightning that crackle against the Poplar's rear shields. The ship shakes. The shields hold. But a larger Elvidian ship—as large as the 118, but black and sharp and sparking with electricity—moves toward us.

"Stay away from those capital ships!" Count Woofbot shouts through comms. "They're slow, but they pack a punch!"

Ari shoots us upward again, firing at nothing and everything as he flies—straight toward the mouth of another Elvidian capital ship. There's nowhere else to go. We're surrounded.

More static. More explosions. Three of our robot

protectors—all ships under Stingy's command—sacrifice themselves by flying straight at an Elvidian ship that's preparing to fire on the station. Its shields crack under the pressure, and all four ships explode.

"How much longer?!" I ask Starlee.

"Only two fewer minutes than the last time you asked!"

In other words: Too long.

"Argh!" Becka shouts, slamming her fist down on the console in front of us. "I can't *believe* this ship only has front-mounted guns! Isn't there anything else we can use to fire?"

"I'm sorry!" Starlee yells back. "We were geologists, not fighters. Even the turrets are just adaptions of old comms tech."

I'm whipped to the side as Ari zigzags to avoid enemy fire. We nearly crash into the 118's shields before the ship yells, "*PULL UP!*" and Ari avoids the collision at the last second. Through the front window, beyond the light speed jamming, another swarm of fighters is detaching from the maw of an Elvidian capital ship. Heading straight for us.

We barely made it through the last wave. We're still *in* the last wave. And now we have only minutes before a new round of Elvidian ships—more than all our remaining ships combined—joins the fray.

Becka groans. "There has to be something else we can do."

"There's not!" Starlee insists as we're hit again. Ari tries to shake a tail by flying extra close to the station's hull and pulling up at the last second. It doesn't work. The fighter's still on us. But the 118's close-range cannons chase it off.

"You can't use the other segments' weapons without detaching them from the convoy," Starlee adds.

Becka freezes where she's sitting. "What do you mean, *the other segments*? What segments?"

"Huh?" Starlee asks back, confused. "The segments." She points up and around. "The Poplar is four segments put together. I mean, we only used this segment to fly. The others are for housing and transport, but they're all capable of detaching and acting as independent shuttles—"

Becka's eyes light up. "Can we fly them remotely?"

Starlee shakes her head. "No."

"Figures," Becka mutters. Without hesitation, she unbuckles her belt and fights Ari's high-flying to stumble to the rear door, grasping at the handholds in the ceiling to keep herself from falling.

"I'm going," she says. "Starlee, send a timer to the other segments so we know how much longer we need to keep this up."

My eyes practically bug out of my head. "What do you mean, you're *going*?"

"You heard her. The Poplar is four ships in one. We can *use* them. If we divide up at the right moment, the

Elvidians might be caught off guard and lose track of which is the main segment. That'll keep Starlee and the scanner safe." She nods at Starlee. "Protect the Poplar. That's our job. We need to give her a fighting chance to run out the clock."

"We're safer together," I protest.

"You gonna order me to stay, Captain?" Her eyes flash. She's not upset. Just driven. She knows what she has to do. "Because I think you owe me a disobeyed order."

I'm still trying to sort out how I feel about this. But Ari doesn't share my hesitation. He pulls a lever and removes his hands from the throttle. "Can you take this?" he asks Starlee.

"No. I mean, yes. I can fly it." She nods. "Of course I can. It's a good plan. Go."

Starlee replaces Ari in the pilot's chair, and Ari joins Becka at the rear of the ship. "I'll take a segment out too."

"You're just going to follow Becka into danger?" I demand.

He shrugs and gives a lopsided grin. "It's worked for me so far," he says and heads out through the door.

I don't know what to do. I don't know if they're right or wrong, or if I'm too scared to know which is which. I'm the captain now, aren't I? I could order them to stay. Maybe they'd listen.

I look behind me at the closed door. I look forward, out the window, at the oncoming next wave of Elvidian fighters. The 118 between us and them, bruised but still holding its ground. In the back of my mind, I'm still thinking about the Minister's advisors. Gone, because of me.

One step at a time.

Take big chances.

Different advice. And also the same: do the right thing.

I unbuckle my belt.

"Wait up," I say. "I'm coming too."

29

"Two minutes until the next wave of fighters gets here," Starlee says.

"Everyone in position?" I ask. We're each in our own segment of the larger Poplar, preparing to detach from each other.

"Roger that, Sigma Leader," Ari says through the comms.

"Wait," Becka says, "I thought *I* was Sigma Leader."

"Yeah, that was when you were captain. Now that Jack's captain again, he's Sigma Leader. You're Sigma One, Starlee is Sigma Two, and I'm Sigma Three."

"Aw," Becka says, like she's genuinely touched. "I'm Sigma One?"

"You're always Sigma One in my book," Ari says.

"Blech," I say. "Can you guys wait until we're dead to talk like that?"

Becka chuckles. "You really know how to put things in perspective, Sigma Leader."

"Let's drop the Sigma thing, okay?" I add. "It's too confusing right now. The Minister knows our names anyway."

Ari sighs but still says, "Aye, aye, Captain."

"One minute," Starlee announces.

I look at my screen. One minute until the next round of fighting. But ten minutes until the scanner finishes its work.

An eternity. And no time at all.

"On my mark," I say, watching the swarm of ships get closer. The gunports on each fighter flicker with the charge of their purple lightning.

My heart beats one thunderous beat.

"Now!" I say, slamming my hand down on the button that depressurizes the airlocks and disconnects the ships. "Detach and burn! Now now now!"

With a thud and a groan, the Poplar comes apart into four identical ships.

"Form up!" I say.

"Jack?!" Principal Lochner calls through the open channel. "What just happened? Are you all right?"

"We're fine," I say, taking the lead. Starlee's right behind me; Ari and Becka flank her sides. "We figured we'd all come out and play. This is the ship Starlee is in." I send him a marker. "That's who you should be protecting. We'll do the same."

Through the audio system, I hear Principal Lochner swallow. "We'll protect *all* of you. Keep the line open.

Stay close to the 118. Lochner out."

And the space around us erupts.

Broken apart, the Poplars are fast ships. Faster, maybe, than the Elvidian fighters. But what they've got in speed, they lack in maneuverability—and firepower. I have no idea how Ari manages those spins. I can barely control a slight turn to one side or the other. I lead the formation straight for the swarm of Elvidian ships, then dive downward when they start firing. But the angle isn't steep enough. The Elvidians easily match course. They hit all of us—Becka's ship twice—with their terrifying lightning cannons.

"Check in!" I yell, abandoning the hope of flying loose, of drawing fire away from both the real Poplar and the 118. If we're going to survive, we need to stay close to home.

"Shields holding," Ari says.

"Same," Starlee agrees.

"Becka?"

A pause. "Yeah. Sorry. I'm fine. Keep going."

I nod even though no one can see me. "Coming about for another run," I say as a squadron of robot ships forms up around us. "Hug the 118 this time."

"Agreed," Ari says with obvious relief. The Elvidian ships must be really slow. The swarm hasn't yet reoriented, and no one has taken potshots at us from behind.

"Okay," I say, tilting to come in directly above the

118's nose cone. I want to position us within range of the rail gun, just in case.

That's when I see them: half the Elvidian fighter force pulling up from the swarm that came at us only seconds ago, heading *away* from the battle.

"Woohoo!" Ari shouts. "They give up easily, don't they?"

Except they don't.

Turning in perfect formation, the Elvidian ships return to battle—heading not for me and the other Poplars, but for the starboard side of the 118. And all the Elvidian ships begin to fire.

Several of the robot ships get off a few rounds of laser fire, picking off an enemy fighter or two. But it's not enough. Within seconds, the robot ships are decimated.

The 118 starts in with its rail gun.

"Turn!" I shout to Principal Lochner. "You've got incoming."

But the 118 stays in line with us.

"*You've* got incoming," he says, picking off one Elvidian fighter at a time. The 118 lights up its close range lasers. But dozens of Elvidian fighters break through, focusing their lightning on a single spot on the 118's shields, firing over and over.

Which is when the should-be invisible shields protecting the 118 glow orange for a moment, the ship screams, "*SHEILDS DOWN!*" and the 118 begins taking fire directly against its hull.

The ship starts turning, starts *tilting*, as the Elvidian weapons peel off the state-of-the-art graphene hull like a knife through butter. One of the 118's engines sputters and dies. Chunks of hull plating fly off into space.

"Diana!" Becka screams. It's so loud in my headset that the speaker crackles. She zags out of formation, cutting across my bow and toward the 118, firing wildly.

I don't know what to do. Starlee is behind me. We still have a few minutes left on the scanner's timer. I can't think. I pull up and try to get a shot or two off on the ships attacking the 118, but they return fire and the ships behind us do the same.

I'm hit.

Shields are still holding. Maybe. My head hits the ceiling. There's a ringing in my ears.

"Becka!" Ari is shouting. "Becka!"

He peels off too, flying helplessly after Becka's ship, which has lost shields and is taking damage to its hull. Its engines are useless. It takes more fire. *I* take more fire. *My* shields are down. The controls at my fingertips spark and go dark. A small flame shoots up from somewhere in my peripheral vision.

Everything is on fire.

The 118.

The Poplars.

The station.

My mind.

And—

Just beyond the light speed jamming, I spot *more* Elvidian ships. Of different shapes and sizes. I imagine the Minister laughing at me. Telling me how useless this fight was. How she can keep this up until we have nothing left and she'll barely notice the losses on her side.

The new ships open fire . . . on the Minister's own capital ships, which shift and return fire.

They're shooting at *each other*.

In an instant, the Elvidian fighters near us retreat, speeding to rejoin their capital ships beyond the light speed jamming. It's hard to understand. Hard to tell who's who. All I see are flashes of light streaking through space like fireworks.

Suddenly it's over. The Minister's ships flee, vanishing in the snap-glow of their light speed engines. Leaving only the newcomers, who hover just past the jamming.

On the open channel, two new figures appear on the holographic interface: one Elvidian, and one—

"Mom?" Starlee says.

Starlee's mother nods, but it's the Elvidian who speaks. His smile adds centuries to the lines already carved through his ancient face. Bale Kontra. "Sorry we're late."

30

"Settle down, settle down," Principal Lochner says, holding up his hands.

It takes a few minutes. More insisting from the principal, some smiles from Ms. Needle and Mr. Cardegna, the usual ice-stare from Mrs. Watts. But eventually, the room goes silent. We're all gathered in the employee break room on the station.

"Thank you," he says, grinning from ear to ear. Now *that's* a real smile. "First, I'd like to thank our hosts for graciously allowing us to settle in on the station while the 118 undergoes repairs. We know you got into this fight for your own freedom, which makes your generosity all the more appreciated. We're eternally grateful for your help and glad to be on the same side."

Admiral Stingy salutes. Its cousin, Z-9B4, promoted it after the battle. Of course, Z-9B4 then promoted *itself* to Grand Admiral, so Stingy's still a rank behind. The row of robots in the back of the room—the admirals,

Creaky, Chucklebot Eight (uploaded into a new body), and Count Woofbot—cheer and hoot and bark.

"Take all the time you need," Admiral Stingy says, clapping Creaky on the back. Creaky's arm doesn't even fall off, which has to be a good sign.

"Next," Principal Lochner continues, "we owe an enormous debt of gratitude to Starlee and her family."

Starlee is sitting with her moms and the rest of the Meerkatians, maybe ten in all. They changed their minds about what we were doing and decided to join us. Apparently, they even headed to the Minister's palace, hoping to help. But by the time they got there, we were gone—and the place was overrun with forces from across the galaxy. Summoned by Bale Kontra's message. By my message. They stormed the palace, freed Bale Kontra, and invited Starlee and her moms to join the fight.

"And of course," Principal Lochner adds, "Bale Kontra."

The Elvidian draws back his hood and lifts a hand. "Please," he says. "I am no longer Bale Kontra, having relinquished my title. Kontra is just fine."

Principal Lochner nods. "Well then, thank you, um, Mr. Kontra, for all your help."

"It is the least I could do," Kontra responds. "And we will continue to help when we can. My forces grow larger every day. More and more decent-hearted Elvidians and other species throughout the League of

Independent Systems are joining our cause. We have vowed to finally bring the secret of the Quarantine out into the open, even if it means fighting against our own leaders. Even the Minister's own former advisors are working with us."

My heart skips a beat. I jolt up out of my seat. "Her advisors? They're alive?"

"They are," he says. "My forces attacked the palace just after the Minister ordered their arrest—and *before* anything worse could occur. Though we could not hold the palace for long, we rescued the advisors and took them with us when we retreated. Thanks to the Minister's heavy hand, they have finally seen through her machinations. Their support will be invaluable."

"So I didn't get them killed?" I say.

"No," he answers, smiling. "In fact, by sending the message that brought my allies to the palace, you saved them."

Relief washes over me as I fall back into my chair, and Bale Kontra—or Kontra, or Mr. Kontra, or whatever—continues: "The Minister will consolidate her forces, no doubt. She does not take defeat lightly. She will strike back, as will the other system leaders allied with her. Nevertheless, for now, we are safe here."

Principal Lochner gulps. "Well, yes. Thank you again."

Over the loudspeakers, the ship says, *"AHEM."* It's patched into the station's comms.

Principal Lochner rolls his eyes. "Calm down, Ship. I'm getting to you. But first, will the following students please join me up front? Jacksonville Graham, Beckenham Pierce, and Arizona Bowman. Mississippi Tinker, Riyadh Windsor, Birmingham Elfbrandt. California Brown, Alem Gena Korematsu, and Indianapolis Pierce."

The nine of us. "Council of Shrew," Ari whispers as we stand to join the principal at the front of the room.

He lifts a short stack of papers up from his podium and shows them off to the school. "For your unparalleled bravery in the face of danger and an unyielding commitment to this school. For your wisdom and kindness. For exemplifying everything the PSS 118 is and can be."

He holds up one of the papers. The top sheet has my name written on it in real ink: *Jacksonville "Jack" Graham*.

"By the powers vested in me as middle-school administrator, I hereby bestow upon each of you the highest honor I can grant: this Principal's Certificate of Achievement."

I make eye contact with Ari and almost crack up. I mean, this is something he gives out every year to kids who, like, "most improved" their grades or helped clean up the classrooms a lot. But I look out at the crowd of fellow students and see no one laughing. Instead, after a moment, Hunter—*Hunter*—stands up and starts a totally unsarcastic slow clap that reverberates around the room into absolutely thunderous applause. When it dies down, and the principal reveals that he printed out a tenth Certificate of Achievement for the 118, the place goes wild.

"*YOU'RE GONNA MAKE AN OLD SHIP CRY,*" it says after a few seconds.

Principal Lochner laughs. "I'm fairly sure ships can't cry."

The ship seems to think about this before saying, "*WELL, I COULD RELEASE A LITTLE AIR RECYCLER COOLANT INTO THE VACUUM OF SPACE. YOU KNOW, FOR EFFECT.*"

That gets the principal laughing even harder. "Maybe another time, okay, Ship?"

"*SUIT YOURSELF.*"

Once we've all sat back down, Missi Tinker raises her hand.

"Yes, Missi?"

"What about"—Missi lowers her voice—"the spy?"

The spy. I'd almost forgotten.

Almost.

Principal Lochner and Chucklebot Eight share a knowing glance, and Principal Lochner explains, "Even before we left Earth, I thought that we had a spy, yes. Someone who sabotaged the 118 and reported back to the Minister's robots." He looks at me. "It's why, before you kids ventured off on your own, I made a show of going along with the robots."

"Wait," Ari says. "You knew the robots were bad the whole time?"

"I had my suspicions, yes. I was concerned that someone on my staff was working with the robots. The bad robots, I mean. So I pretended to trust *everyone*, because I feared I couldn't trust anyone. I hoped that if I played innocent and kept my eyes open, the traitor would let down their guard enough for me to find out who it was."

Ari elbows me in the side. "Told you he had it under control."

Principal Lochner shakes his head. "But I was wrong. We recently concluded a full diagnostic of the ship, using every resource available on this station. It turns out that the 118 was infected with a computer virus that may have been planted months ago, possibly while we were imprisoned on Elvid IV this summer. That virus seems to have been what was disrupting our systems, and it may also have been transmitting data offship. It was, in essence, the spy. We've purged the malware, however, and . . ."

"*I'VE GOT A CLEAN BILL OF HEALTH*," the ship announces.

"I'm sorry for not being open with you kids." Principal Lochner turns back to the teachers. "I'm sorry I doubted you. We're all in this together. Which brings us to our next step."

The room quiets down.

"Thanks to Starlee's extraordinary machine," Principal Lochner says seriously, "we have this."

Mr. Cardegna dims the lights and raises a slowly spinning hologram of the galaxy above our heads.

"One line," the principal says. In red, it crosses the galaxy from one end to the other. "And another." In green, it starts in the Orion Arm—in our solar system—and connects with the red line somewhere beyond the galactic center.

"X marks the spot," I whisper from the front row.

"This is where the trail leads," Principal Lochner explains. "Bale—er, Mr. Kontra? Or, can I just call you Mr. K?"

The former member of the Minister's secret alien council nods and tells us, "Mr. K is fine." He twirls a finger, another signal to whoever is controlling the map. It zooms in on the spot where the two lines connect. "We have sent automated scouts to this precise location, where there apparently rests an enormous, lonely planet."

"Lonely planet?" Becka whispers to Ari.

"He means a planet without a star. Just floating around in space, nothing around it."

Becka puts an arm around Diana, who's sitting on her left. "Sad."

"This planet is uncharted," Bale Kontra—*Mr. K?*—continues, "which is curious."

"Are they there?" Hunter calls out from a few rows back. "Is everyone there?"

"No," Mr. K answers, bursting that barely formed bubble of hope. "We do not believe so. Our readings detected no life signs on what we are calling Planet X. And, despite its size, the planet would be too small to hold your entire species, let alone others."

Terrified chatter buzzes through the room.

Are we too late?

Did we lose?

Was this all for nothing?

Principal Lochner stands up tall. "There's more."

"Correct," Mr. K says. "Much more. Mysterious patterns on the surface. Odd readings from beneath the surface. There is something unique about Planet X."

"We're hopeful that we'll learn something valuable there," Principal Lochner tells us. "so we'll repair the 118 and head out." He looks at us kids, at Starlee's parents, at the robot army leaders, and at Mr. K. "Together."

We all clap for that, but he's not done. "You've been so strong, despite everything we've lost. I want you to think about that for a moment—what you've managed to accomplish. I know that it's hard to dwell on the present sometimes. Especially when everything we're fighting for—finding our families, bringing them home—is still in the future. We're aiming to complete the *next* mission. Climb the *next* mountain."

"Kick the next Elvidian butt!" Hunter shouts.

The room cracks up. But Principal Lochner looks at Mr. K and goes still. "Sorry," he says to our Elvidian ally.

"By all means," Mr. K says. "Let us, as you say, kick butt."

Which gets the room going so loud, you'd think Chucklebot Eight was putting on another set. Principal Lochner slaps Mr. K on the back like they've known each other their whole lives.

"But seriously. We've done something incredible. All of us here. We don't know what's coming next, but right now, I want all of you to close your eyes."

Another cheesy Principal Lochner assembly closer. Somehow, I've actually missed these. A bit of nervous laughter bounces around the room. More than a little eye rolling. But Principal Lochner pushes on.

"Come on," he says. "Humor me. If you can fight monsters and aliens and robots, you can go along with my nonsense."

Ari and Becka close their eyes, and I do too.

"I want you to take a moment. Think about something or someone you have. Now. Here. Not in the future. Right now. Something you're proud of. Someone you're grateful for."

My mind cycles through the last few months. Using my dad's light speed engine to get away from the Quarantine. Escaping from Elvidian jail. Refueling the 118 and making it back to Earth. Getting through the robot civil war and Hunter's coup. Finding the Great Library. Surviving another showdown with the Minister. Incredible, impossible things.

But not what I'm most proud of.

With our eyes still closed, Ari puts an arm around

my shoulders. Becka, on my other side, does the same. And I wrap my own arms around them both. Around my friends. My *someones*. In a weird way, despite everything we've lost, we've also found something awesome.

"Okay," Principal Lochner says. "Open your eyes."

He's standing there, his arms crossed at his chest, his eyes glassy. I look from side to side and behind me, at the rows of other kids. Who all have their arms around each other. All of us. An unbroken chain.

"Do you know what I'm most proud of? Most grateful for?" He pauses. "All of you."

* * *

The assembly ended an hour ago, but we're still here, on the station. The crew's repairing the 118's environmental controls, so we'll be offship for at least another week. Ari's calling it our shore leave. We've got run of the station, mostly. Except for the areas undergoing repairs or where the grown-ups have set up their command headquarters. It's a relief to have them back in charge. To go back to being a kid.

"You're sure it's not *cyclopses*?" Missi asks as we walk.

Riya grunts. "No way. It's *cyclopsi* for sure."

"Sorry," Ari insists. "It's just *cyclops*. Like how you pluralize fish. One fish, two fish. So one cyclops. Two cyclops. Like that."

"But what if you're facing two different *types* of cyclops?" I ask. "Is it cyclopses then?"

Becka: "Can we stay focused, please?"

We're exploring the warehouse, where the old robot emperor's "throne room" used to be. Technically, we're here to take inventory—and got a bit distracted when we passed a shelf of decommissioned cyclops . . . es.

There's a lot of cool stuff in here. As we wander down the aisles, we debate the best way to set up a makeshift student lounge in case the 118's out of order for longer than expected. Everyone's got a different idea. Diana wants to rig up a virtual gaming center, even if it'll be a lot of work. Becka and Hunter—on the same side of a debate for once—are pushing for a zero-g basketball court. That probably won't be too complicated—if we can convince the robots to slow down one of the station's rotating gravitational rings.

"I don't know," I say, pulling some art supplies down from a shelf. Paint. Paintbrushes. Sketchbooks. There's a large easel a quarter of the way up. Becka could reach it if she stretches. "Maybe something . . . low key?"

Everyone stares blankly at me for a second before going back to the discussion.

Becka: ". . . already got a basketball from the ship and—"

Riya: ". . . think we should still be practicing security drills, in case—"

Missi: ". . . get back to classes as soon as we possibly—"

Ari: ". . . don't see why we wouldn't want to look into upgrades for Doctor's Shrew's—"

"Mr. Graham?" Mrs. Watts calls from the end of the aisle.

"Oooooo-ooo-ooooooh," some of kids chant. The universal jingle for *you're in trouble*. Ordinarily, they'd be right: Fifty percent of Mrs. Watts's job is giving kids detention. But I just helped save, you know, everyone. Again. And I can't think of a reason why I'd be in trouble now. So I shrug, tell Ari and Becka to at least grab a set of watercolors for me, and follow Mrs. Watts out into the corridor.

"What'd I do this time?" I ask, trying to joke around. I've never had a jokey relationship with Mrs. Watts. Probably because Mrs. Watts has never made a joke in her entire life. But we're on a space station with a robot army and a bunch of aliens—so stranger things have happened.

Mrs. Watts doesn't answer. Instead, she takes me deeper into the station, to a section that I could've sworn was closed off for repairs. But the door is unlocked, and she leads me inside.

Immediately, I know something's wrong. This place *is* closed off for repairs. A valve by my feet is spewing yellow steam into the air. On the far wall, one of the station's temporary airlocks has been welded over a section of missing hull, barely sealing off the room from the vacuum of space beyond. There's a weird *tick tick tick*ing noise and—behind me—a *thud*. I turn. Mrs. Watts has closed the door behind us. Locked it. Removed a small blaster from . . . from where? And why? Unless—

"You?" I ask her.

She reaches into the hair on the back of her head and . . . pulls a lever? Her eyes—her regular, human, brown eyes—change colors. Turn silvery and metallic. Her scalp pops open with a hiss, revealing wires and flashing lights and—

"You're a robot."

Mrs. Watts smiles. And I'm hit with the irony of her only acting human *after* revealing that she's something else. "These days," Mrs. Watts says, "it's hard to tell the difference between inferior biological organisms and machines."

"So there *was* a spy," I breathe.

"Oh yes. Me. Watching. Waiting. Nudging things along."

I try to sound tough. Sound like I'm not terrified. But coming face to face with the real Mrs. Watts is somehow scarier than confronting the Minister. "Well, your nudging hasn't worked very well. We keep escaping. We keep winning."

Half-headless Mrs. Watts shrugs. "We'll see."

"Who are you, though, really?" I ask as she twists her hair back on. "What do you want?"

"Irrelevant," is all she answers. "Goodbye."

Mrs. Watts reaches behind her, stretching her right arm around in a more twisted angle than an arm should ever twist. She unlocks the door and—blaster trained on me the whole time—slips back out the way she came. I hear the clanking sound of a bolt turning as she locks me in.

I run to the door and bang. Try to turn the locked handle. Try to pull the door off its hinges. I activate my comm ring. No signal. Reach for my Pencil. It's not in my pocket. How's it not there?

"Hey! Help! Someone help me! Please!"

Footsteps behind me. I'm not alone. And the voice— the impossible voice—calls out to me.

"Jack."

The skin on my arms and legs erupts with goose-bumps. Tears pool in my eyes. The voice is as familiar as my own. Because I've heard it my whole life.

I turn around. "Mom?"

"Hi, sweetie," she says.

"What . . . ? What are you doing here?" Before she can respond, I get my bearings. "No, it isn't you. It *can't* be you. This is another trick. Like Mrs. Watts. Or Orientation."

"Do you think you're inside a simulation?" she asks.

"I . . . I don't know."

"Do I look like a fake?" She takes another step forward.

I trip backward, but I've got nowhere to go, pressed up against the cold steel door.

"No," I admit. It's her. Or at least, it looks like her.

Feels like her. "But that doesn't mean anything. Mrs. Watts didn't look like a fake either." I pause, rethinking. "Mostly."

My mom—no, *not* my mom; it can't be—nods and walks closer. "Would a fake know that we let you walk outside the residential dome when you were six? Even though you were technically too scrawny to pass the weight checks for spacewalk regs? Those walks always calmed you down. Would a fake know that, for the briefest period before you turned ten, you wanted so badly to be an entymologist?"

"Ants are cool," is all I can say as I wipe my eyes.

"Ants *are* cool," she agrees. "Would a fake know that we gave you the master bedroom in our apartment, because it had the biggest window looking out at the moonscape? But that it didn't make your claustrophobia any better until your dad rigged up his old telescope—so that you could see so much more than what was right in front of you?"

"I don't . . . I don't understand," I say, allowing her to take my hands in hers. They feel human—and exactly like I remember them, down to small calluses on her left hand. She gets those from repeatedly restarting to teach herself guitar before stopping again a few days later. "How are you here? Where's everyone else? Where's Dad?"

She shakes her head, as if to tell me that those aren't the right questions, even though they're the *only* questions. I pull my hands back, suddenly furious at her. For leaving. For showing up now, without any answers.

"I'm sorry," she tells me. "For everything. I love you, Jackie. I'm so proud of you. And I promise to explain everything when we get there."

My mouth drops open, but all the things I want to say don't get said:

I'm not going anywhere with you.

I haven't forgiven you.

This can't be real.

Instead, she extends a hand again, and I take it.

"Come with me," my mom says, leading me across the room. I finally notice the small ship that's berthed outside the temporary airlock. "There's something you need to see."

ARI'S LOG: DAY 8

I've started my count over. Now, I'm marking the amount of time that's passed since Jack went missing. Until he comes back, nothing else matters. Not to me, anyway. We've looked for him everywhere. Turned the station, the 118, and every ship in the sector upside down. But nothing.

And since then, us kids have been on lockdown. Robot guards posted at all exits to the ship. We have access to the dorms, the mess hall, the gym—and that's it. To help "keep order," Principal Lochner's promoted Mr. Cardeqna and Mrs. Watts to Co-Assistant Principals and given them priority access to all systems. After everything that's happened, I think this is most panicked I've ever seen the principal.

It's like—losing the whole human race: That was manageable. Losing a single student: That was when the world really ended.

Where are you, Jack?

ARI'S LOG: DAY 12

We had an assembly today. The ship is repaired. We're good to go. Mr. K says we're running out of time before the Minister comes for us. Mrs. Watts apparently voted to stay as long as it takes to find Jack. She doesn't want to leave the system without him. Who even knew she had a heart? She's all right in my book now.

But Principal Lochner and the other teachers disagree with her. They don't think it's safe here anymore. They think we need to move on. Head to Planet X without my best friend in the whole universe.

And you know the worst part? I think they're right.

ARI'S LOG: DAY 14

Today's the day. Our next mission. We're pretty upbeat, all things considered. Who knows what we'll find? I'm trying to think on the bright side: Maybe Jack's there already? Maybe he found another light speed engine and used it to start the mission early? I don't know why he'd do that. Especially without Becka and me. We're the dream team, right?

I also don't want to think about any of the other possibilities. Except that's all I can think about: Jack, tied up, dangling above a pool of genetically engineered sharks while the Minister cackles. Jack, lost in some parallel universe, where Principal Lochner has a mustache and is evil, Becka is bad at sports, and Hunter uses words like "please" and "thank you." Jack, dead.

We're leaving behind a package for him on the station in case he comes back. A new Pencil. Enough rations to last a year. A biometric key to a light-speed-equipped Poplar segment that we're stashing in the main hangar, complete with the map to Planet X. And two short video messages—one from me, one from Becka. She bawled the whole way through recording hers. Didn't even try to pretend she wasn't crying. So you know she's worried.

So am I. But I have to focus on the mission. That's what Jack would want me to do. Besides, I don't need to be this worried. If there ever was a kid in this whole galaxy who could survive on their own, lost in space . . . well . . . that kid's probably Becka Pierce. But if there were ever <u>two</u> kids who could survive on their own, Jack would for sure score second place.

ARI'S LOG: MESSAGE TRANSCRIPT

Hang in there, Jack. I don't know if you're on Planet X, or if someone's taken you somewhere else. But we'll find you. I'm not going to give up. Becka's not gonna give up. We're not going to let anyone forget you're missing. We're going to turn every rock in this universe upside down until we find you, okay? We found the Poplar. We found Planet X. We'll find you too. So hold on. Because we're coming. I promise. And may Sol burn brightly till the end.

ACKNOWLEDGMENTS

Let's switch it up.

First but not least: Henry. Sorry I didn't include you the last time around. In my defense, you weren't born yet. But that's no excuse, time machines being what they are (or, presumably, what they will be). You're so curious and sweet, and I'm so glad you joined us. Also, sorry I inadvertently taught you to laugh like Jabba the Hutt. I feel like that'll come in handy eventually.

Next, as long as I'm here, Serena. My best bug in the whole wide world. (And galaxy and universe and multiverse.) I want to think that I inherited at least a bit of your creativity and kindness and ingenuity. I can't wait for all the stories you and your brother are going to tell. Save a few for me, will you?

And Tali. Making space (ha!) for me to write—at this point—over 100,000 words about alien sea monsters and stand-up comedian robots isn't always easy, I know. (See supra Henry & Serena, et al.) Thank you. Seriously.

If you ever get the hankering to, say, draft a yarn about some eighteenth-century Scottish bed and breakfast (with a secret!), let me know. I'll take the kids to Van Saun.

I'm especially grateful, as always, to my agent, Elana Roth Parker, without whom Jack, Becka, and Ari would still be (cryogenically?) hibernating in a drawer somewhere. I went back to read my original query for Book 1. And a week after I sent Elana the full manuscript, she mused that it felt like *"Hitchhiker's Guide* meets *Wayside School."* I've tried to keep channeling that energy in Book 2.

To the team at Lerner/Carolrhoda—an equally big thanks. As Ari (and I) would say around Passover time, if I'd only gotten to tell one story in this series, *dayenu*. That I get to tell another, well, I'm over the moon. For the *fact* of the book, sure. But also for the village I know it takes, including star book designer Kimberly Morales, production designer Erica Johnson, and editor-extraordinaire Amy Fitzgerald. If you're wondering whether an editor for these kinds of books engages in philosophical debates about the politics of robot revolution or validating discussions about the narrative utility of a Chekhov's jetpack, well, wonder no more. It's an affirmative, Captain. Thanks, Amy.

I'm a little embarrassed, because I didn't thank him in Book 1. But Petur Antonsson, wow. The cover for *Seventh Grade vs. the Galaxy* is indispensable to the book, and the same is true this time around.

And my law firm. As in, the one I "day job" work for. It was not a foregone conclusion that you would support me in this as kindly as you have—I realize that my, um, middle-grade-space-opera writing doesn't exactly translate to a better motion to dismiss. But you all value your colleagues as people, and that isn't lost on me. Pete, I promise to have that brief on your desk in the morning.

Finally, as I'm writing this after the end of my debut year, I also wanted to take the opportunity to thank my fellow MG #novel19s, for their wisdom and inspiration and friendship. Nicole Melleby, my Garden State buddy. (I'm not 100 percent sure whether *Eighth Grade vs. the Machines* is the only middle grade science fiction novel to open in Newark, New Jersey. But it's gotta be a short list, right?) And my JPST family in particular. In alphabetical order (because they're all equally the best): Chris Baron, Cory Leonardo, Gillian McDunn, Jessica Kramer, Naomi Milliner, Nicole Panteleakos, and Rajani LaRocca. My 2019 wouldn't have been the same without you. Or my 2018. Or my 2020.

Oh, 2020. I'm writing this in May and it's . . . a mixed bag, isn't it? To say the least. But I guess that's the point of all this. To thank you all for making my 2020 that much brighter.

(2021 Update: Ditto.)

ABOUT THE AUTHOR

Joshua S. Levy is a husband, lawyer, father, and children's book author who lives in New Jersey. He is also the author of *Seventh Grade vs. the Galaxy*. Learn more at https://www.joshuasimonlevy.com.

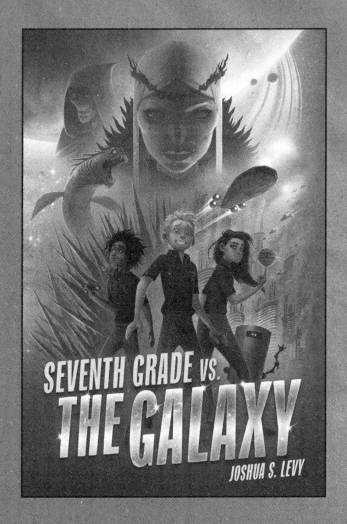